THE BALTIMORE ATROCITIES

— A NOVEL —

John Dermot Woods

COFFEE HOUSE PRESS

MINNEAPOLIS • 2014

COPYRIGHT © 2014 John Dermot Woods
COVER AND BOOK DESIGN by Linda Koutsky
ILLUSTRATIONS © John Dermot Woods
AUTHOR PHOTOGRAPH © Dave Brown

Coffee House Press books are available to the trade through our primary distributor, Consortium Book Sales & Distribution, cbsd.com or (800) 283-3572. For personal orders, catalogs, or other information, write to: info@coffeehousepress.org.

Coffee House Press is a nonprofit literary publishing house. Support from private foundations, corporate giving programs, government programs, and generous individuals helps make the publication of our books possible. We gratefully acknowledge their support in detail in the back of this book.

Visit us at coffeehousepress.org.

LIBRARY OF CONGRESS CIP INFORMATION
Woods, John Dermot, 1977– author illustrator.
The Baltimore Atrocities : a novel / by John Dermot Woods.
pages cm
ISBN 978-1-56689-371-8 (paperback)
ISBN 978-1-56689-379-4 (ebook)
1. Baltimore (Md.)—Fiction. I. Title.
PS3623.O6764B35 2014
813'.6—dc23
2014006993
PRINTED IN THE UNITED STATES
FIRST EDITION | FIRST PRINTING

FOR THOMAS BERNHARD AND THE OTHER GHOSTS WHO
HAUNT THE PLACES THEY HATED TO LOVE

1

THOSE WHO HAVE LOST SOMETHING IMPORTANT, like a mother or a father, or a brother or a sister, before they have a sense of themselves, must face maturity as seekers, constantly distracted by glimpses of things that are lost, with the hope that those things might be recovered. These people, people like my companion and me, have no choice but to chase fleeting visions, because, until they can be fixed and defined, our consciences will be wracked by a constant and grating sense of incompleteness.

We met in biology lab during our sophomore year at the city science and engineering high school. We were both excellent students (a requirement for admission into the school), but neither of us cared much for science or engineering. We did our work and received respectable grades, but we had inner lives that were lived somewhere far away from our classrooms. Little did we know at the time, but both of our minds were occupied by the same place: Baltimore.

One late autumn afternoon, I was staring out the window, watching dark shadows stretch across the blacktop playing fields that were used by the school's intramural-only sports programs. I always studied empty public spaces closely, sure that something obvious was waiting for me to find it. I was distracted by the laughter of Karen DiBiasi. She sat on a stool at the lab bench before me. I immediately noticed how her posture pulled her jeans down just enough—and T-shirt up just enough—to reveal the small of her back and the top of her underwear. Lost in a fifteen-year-old's reverie, I was embarrassed to realize that my teacher, an old man whose name I now forget, was calling my name again and again; this, in fact, was why Karen DiBiasi was laughing.

"Mr. Austin, would you be so kind as to make room for Thomas at your lab bench? You need a partner for this work, like everyone else."

I shoved over silently. A tall and almost impossibly thin boy sat on the stool beside me. I saw his eyes fall on that same band of pale pink cotton and paler pink skin before them, only to float to the dusky schoolyard outside. His eyes also seemed ready to find whatever was waiting for him out there.

The teacher droned his instructions, a handwritten overhead projection redundantly describing that day's lab procedure, a standard frog dissection. Neither of us reached for the hermetically wrapped scalpel, each deferring to the other. Finally, I nodded and said, "You go."

He unwrapped the tool and gently nudged the skin of the frog pinned to the dish before him. I watched as he slowly cut from below the frog's mouth to where its legs met, releasing a torsoful of tiny organs. He made another deft crosswise cut and the frog's insides spilled across the petri dish. The cuts were so clean that the corpse seemed completely undisturbed by its evisceration (which, of course, a dead body would be). I watched as he used the scalpel to draw the organs across the petri dish, creating a Rorschach pattern of bloodstains and flesh. It was beautiful in an unqualified sense.

Suddenly the tray, and frog and innards with it, was pulled away. Our elderly teacher held it before us and glared. "Outrageous!" he said. "This is outrageous frog slaughter."

"But—" my partner said.

"But what, Mr. Specter?"

"How is it slaughter if the frog is already dead?"

Ignoring this, the teacher turned to me. "And you just watched? You just *observed* this perversion?"

I nodded. I thought the word *perversion* was accurate. I was fascinated by the coldness with which Thomas had handled the messy organs.

"Leave. Now." The teacher dropped the frog and tray in the trash. He picked up the scalpel and pointed it at us. "You and you, leave now."

And so we did, gathering our books without protest, watched silently by our peers, exiting unhurried and unembarrassed. Out in the hall by ourselves, neither of us spoke. He turned left toward the library, and I turned right toward the cafeteria for a late lunch. Hot dogs and chicken fingers were my favorite menu items in those days.

NEW JERSEY

IN THE SUBURBS OF NEW YORK CITY, the police were called to detain a trespasser who had been witnessed climbing the fences of several residents' backyards and digging up their lawns with a steel shovel. The trespasser was a woman, a mother who said she was investigating the yards because she felt sure she'd discover the entrance to an underground tunnel leading directly to Manhattan, a tunnel in which she believed her daughter was trapped. (As you can imagine, her story particularly captured our attention.) Her daughter had gone missing the previous year, as was well documented by Baltimore County police and well publicized by the Maryland media when, on a field trip to Gunpowder Falls State Park, she ran away from the class and presumably drowned in the Gunpowder River, which was overrun with early spring snowmelt. As Gunpowder Falls State Park is clearly located in central Maryland (one of the New Jersey police officers had even spent a day hiking there the previous summer), the police questioned the sad mother—whose torn clothing, rat's nest of hair, and pungent smell suggested weeks or even months of neglect of personal hygiene— about her true intentions in prowling through these quiet backyards. They were additionally suspicious because a quick background check revealed that the woman had a criminal record. She was once a successful landscape architect who had, many years earlier, served a short prison sentence for illegally investing funds that she had collected as treasurer of her Episcopal church. Still, it appeared that her actions were the product of honest delusion, and so the police and the victims of her digging spree agreed that no good would come of pressing charges.

THE CLOSING OF THE FACULTY LOUNGE

B ACK IN THE SIXTIES, at a junior high school in Roland Park, as the story goes, a student passed a note in chemistry class the day before the final exam; in response, her teacher cut off her right pinkie with a scalpel. Apparently, the homely chemistry teacher was an object of derision for not only his students, but for his fellow faculty members as well. Just that morning in the faculty lounge, he had suffered the humiliating injustice of having some foreign substance (orange juice and salt?) put into his morning coffee while his back was turned. Of course, he didn't notice until after he took his first sip, already sitting in his laboratory classroom, and he heard adult laughter follow immediately from the hallway. The school day was about to begin and he had no time to replenish his cup. When he caught his student passing a note, he quietly called her to the front of the room and removed a classroom-use scalpel from its hermetically sealed package. Before she could turn to smirk at the other students, he had removed her finger. While she screamed, he locked the door and told the class that whoever else had written on the note he was holding in his hand would likewise lose a finger. He opened the note to find a list of insults directed at him, written in the distinct handwriting of fifteen of the class's twenty-four students. He cut off twelve more right pinkies and two left pinkies before walking out of the school that morning. A sign still hangs on the door of the faculty lounge, informing beleaguered teachers that the room is out of service until further notice.

LAB TESTS

A TEACHER RETURNED AFTER ONLY FIFTEEN MINUTES of searching for a child who had gone missing on a school field trip to the nature center. She ran into the center's administrative office still shuddering at what she had just seen. She said that she had found the child sitting on a bed of pine needles, and no sooner had she arrived than she noticed a black bear (which was common in the region, but rarely seen so close to humans), standing quietly behind her student. The teacher said she quickly ran for the child, but, in doing so, frightened her, causing her to scream, which, in turn, spooked the bear. The bear reacted quickly and violently: it swatted at the child and proceeded to maul her, so, helpless, the teacher fled to safety. An immediate search for the girl (or evidence of her death) proved fruitless. After another day's search, they pronounced her dead and her parents made funeral arrangements. They asked the teacher to eulogize their daughter at the service, which she did, exhibiting great passion and pain. At the end of the school year, the teacher resigned and moved away from Baltimore. Although she broke off contact with all her friends and colleagues, it is believed she moved to either Tucson, Arizona, or Boise, Idaho. Two years later, during our time in Baltimore, a hiker on the trails near the nature center uncovered the well-decomposed body of a girl. The medical examiner determined that the body had suffered serious physical trauma, but it was trauma too mild to have been inflicted by a bear; it appeared the child had been beaten and perhaps strangled by a human. Lab tests proved the body was certainly that of the student whom the teacher claimed to have seen mauled to death before her very eyes.

ROLE MODEL

THE SECONDARY SCHOOLS TRUANCY OFFICER is the most misnamed and miserable position available in the city civil service, and, because of the service that truancy officers are actually able to provide, one can only hold the position for a brief period unless he hopes to bring frustration and disappointment home to his family's dinner table every night. The unlikely, the all-too-likely, the infuriating, and the deadening are presented on his case list each morning, and, as he must earn his paycheck by confronting each of these concerns, he refuses to feel moved by any particular one of them. A friend of mine, who bravely held this position for almost two years, shared with me only one story from his time on the job, as it must have seemed remarkable compared to the other events he witnessed. Moskowitz, a principal of a high school south of the harbor for many years (and an outspoken supporter of progressive educational policy throughout the city), after learning that a student whom he had personally mentored (and whom he thought he had *saved*) rarely attended school and was linked to various criminal activities, said that he had no choice but to expel the young man, who had been an all-city point guard just the previous year. Following the student's expulsion, Moskowitz declared that he had to do something that made a real difference. After this bold proclamation, he returned to his office and shut the pebbled glass of the door behind him. His staff listened compassionately to the sobs and then silence that came from his office. Only when they opened the door hours later did they learn that what they had thought was crying was the principal choking on the rope with which he had hanged himself.

2

M Y MOTHER WAS LATE PICKING ME UP from school on the day we dissected the frog. I sat on the parking lot curb and waited for her to come from the dentist's office, where she managed the appointment schedule and billing. It was early evening but almost totally dark out. Still, the high school parking lot was flooded with sodium vapor light. I noticed a shadow perched on the curb a few hundred feet away. Soon I saw that it was my new lab partner. I couldn't tell if he had noticed me. Both of us sat and watched as headlights swept into the lot, paused (usually followed by the slam of a car door), and swept out again. This happened again and again without our respective rides arriving.

After fifteen minutes or so, a group of chattering girls exited the school's front doors. I turned my head away instinctively and waited for them to pass. Their chatter quieted, but I could feel their singular presence still on the sidewalk. Then, a lone voice: "You're disgusting." Karen DiBiasi. I turned, more confused than offended. I had never been insulted, let alone addressed so directly by one of my classmates. But I soon saw that Karen's words were not meant for me. She stood over my lab partner, scowling at him. No one had noticed me.

He looked up at her and nodded, then put his head down. He continued to wait. His even keel obviously angered Karen more. His perversion was bad enough, but his nonchalance at having it acknowledged cut to the heart of her very understanding of the way things should be. "I said," she said, "you're disgusting. You should know that." Her friends' eyes joined hers in a silent chorus of scorn. He slid down the curb a few feet.

"What you did to that frog was wrong. You think that impresses people, rubbing frog guts around? Do you think anyone even cared?"

"You did," I found myself speaking aloud.

Karen jumped, startled by my presence. "You," she whispered. "I've seen you. I've seen you looking . . ." Her voice fell away.

"You cut up the same dead frog as he did," I said. "The difference is, you followed an instruction sheet. My friend"—he looked up in surprise—"on the other hand, made something."

Another set of headlights rolled into the lot. It was Karen's ride. Her friends filed into the back of the car, heads shaking in disapproval. Karen placed her hand on the door handle and paused, looking at me, then back at my companion. "You," she said. "You're disgusting."

"I'm sure I am."

She opened the door and got into the car without another word. The car pulled off and we sat alone once again. Now it seemed like more effort to ignore the other's presence than to acknowledge it.

I looked out into the almost-empty lot. The fluorescence above turned the bushes along the edge into an artificial green fence, beyond which was blackness. My mother was never this late. Even though I was older, she constantly feared she might lose me, that I might disappear into the darkness, as her daughter once did.

"It's getting dark so early." He had moved beside me. "The shadows really intensify this time of year. I like that."

"Right. It's like there's more possibility. Something's hidden, which means something can be found."

He nodded. We both looked at the bushes. I thought I saw a branch move. I concentrated on the spot, but could detect nothing. Then the edges of the shadow were torn open by another set of headlights. It was my mother's car. She pulled up and I stood slowly. Opening the passenger-side door, I looked back at my lab partner. "Do you have a ride?"

"Probably not."

"Want one?"

He got in the car and my mother and I returned him to the safety of his home that night.

HIGH HOPES

S HORTLY AFTER RETURNING from a tragic summer vacation in the Poconos, a man in Towson filed for divorce from his wife because, one afternoon, while out on a pontoon boat alone with their two daughters, she saved the wrong daughter, in his opinion, when both daughters, neither of whom knew how to swim, fell into the lake. She saved the ten-year-old, whom he felt he had already lost, and not the six-year-old, for whom he had high hopes. During the divorce proceedings, he was asked what these high hopes were exactly, and he said that he expected that she would be strong willed and clear of purpose and understand the weakness of her mother, and would have inflicted on that woman whatever justice was fitting and proper.

LIKE MY MOTHER

T O EXPLAIN WHY HIS MOTHER HAD KILLED HIS FATHER, a promising chef in Mount Vernon (who bought his morning newspaper at the same store I did and, as time went on, became possessed by the frantic pace and improvisational nature of his job) reasoned that his father had been such a consummate caretaker of his children that his mother had been deprived of her identity and her ability to be admired and even loved by her children, which reminded me of my own mother, who had at least an aspect of her maternal duty stolen from her. Still, my mother never killed anyone, let alone my father.

DAYCARE

S EVERAL YEARS BEFORE OUR TIME in the neighborhood, a woman named
Maureen "Mo" Richards lived in our very house and opened a daycare
on the bottom two floors. Before she even opened for business, word spread
that she had left New Jersey for Baltimore because a child had choked to
death on a baby carrot at the previous daycare she had managed. There
were also persistent rumors of sexual abuse charges that had been filed
against her. Despite the lack of evidence, no parents were willing to leave
their child in the woman's care, even in a neighborhood where children
were abundant and daycare options were scarce, and so, despite her wise
choice of location, the woman's business was an abject failure, forcing her
to shut down and sell her home to my companion's uncle, at a loss. Over
time, our neighbors concluded that the rumors about the woman were
completely baseless and, in fact, were malicious lies spread by another local
daycare owner, Ms. Alessi, hoping to gain a competitive advantage. Ms.
Alessi recently reported that while attending a trade conference in Cincin-
nati, she learned the fate of her failed competitor: she had moved back to
New Jersey and is said to have drowned in the ocean, the whispered explanation being that it was an act of suicide.

TWO PRINCIPALS

TWO HIGH SCHOOL PRINCIPALS who managed underfunded and academically underperforming schools on opposite sides of the city—one in the west and one in the east—agreed, in an effort to "shake up" their respective student bodies, to have their morning buses rerouted to the other's school. The decision was made while eating room-temperature hot dogs bought from a street vendor, and they consulted neither the school board nor the students' parents. However, both principals mentioned their planned arrangement to their spouses, and rumors of the flip-flop spread. On the Sunday evening before the Monday that the buses were to be rerouted, police officers visited the quiet homes of both men. They were both detained (though neither was formally arrested). In an extreme case of "teaching someone a lesson," the school principal from the east was sent to the penitentiary on the west side, and the principal from the west was placed in the general population of a jail on the east side; the geographic switch was to avoid the dangerous business of being incarcerated with former students. The Department of Education made sure that no mention of the principals appeared in the newspaper or on the nightly news. On Monday morning, the buses took the students to the same schools they always took them to. The kids sat in (or avoided) the same classrooms they were assigned to every day, and the principals' wives both opened their mailboxes to find their husbands' letters of termination.

SHELDON WEATHERS

SITTING ON THE SMALL PATCH OF PUBLIC GRASS was a young boy whose sweatshirt bore the name of a local elementary school, although he said he was from Modesto, California. My neighbors, who eventually brought him into their living room (he seemed lost and afraid standing outside), dismissed his story as a childhood invention. The boy—whose homework worksheet, which they found in his backpack, identified him as Sheldon Weathers—explained that his real name was George and in June, right after school had let out, he had boarded a bus from Modesto to Phoenix, then to Chicago by way of Denver, and finally to Baltimore (after having spent an afternoon in Washington, DC). In August, right before the new school year was set to begin, he said that he had returned to Modesto, but sitting in a classroom in California on the cusp of fourth grade, he realized that he had no desire to stay in Modesto, so he left school immediately and set out on another days-long Greyhound trip, retracing his steps to Baltimore. My neighbors called the police, who responded immediately and, after about an hour, with just a few phone calls confirmed that the boy's story was completely accurate. (This made my companion and I wonder if our own missing siblings had not been abducted as we'd always assumed, but perhaps absconded by their own volition.) The police also learned that at seven years old, the boy had shot and killed his father, a physically abusive man, and that the court had deemed it best for him to live with his aunt far away in Baltimore. Social services records suggested that even in his new home, Sheldon, as he was newly christened by his aunt, was a victim of abuse; this time the abuse was neglect.

3

TWO BOILED HOT DOGS CRADLED IN FOIL, each topped with ketchup, no mustard, and a bag of Wise potato chips sat before me. I sucked on a drink box of iced tea and waited for my companion. When he arrived, he placed his meal on the table: five chicken fingers, coated in bread crumbs just dry enough to cling, arranged around a deep pool of honey mustard. He too sucked on a drink box of iced tea. As soon as he sat, I, raised to be polite, began to eat.

He laid a pink carbon duplicate on the table. "Midterm report," he said, tapping the form.

"Bio lab?"

"Passing, somehow."

I pulled a similar pink form from my back pocket. "Me too. A B+, believe it or not."

He chewed his chicken and scanned the lunchroom. It was a calm day, with most of the other students reading large textbooks as they ate, the recreation of a science and engineering school. "It looks like we're going to get out of here on time."

I knew I should be excited by the prospect of a prompt graduation, but, as I took the first bite out of my second hot dog, I couldn't bear to consider what would happen to me once I was released from the cocoon of secondary education. To me, traveling meant getting lost, which meant never coming back. "Yeah, but once we're out, where do we go?"

My friend crushed the drink box in his hand. Iced tea dribbled down the side. "I don't know really."

I studied my midterm report. I had received an A in phys ed and an A in studio art. "Gym and art, my two best subjects. I suppose I'm taking advantage of the curve."

"Baltimore, maybe."

"What?"

"Baltimore," my companion said. "It's the only place I've ever thought of going. Maybe not right after I graduate. But one day, I'll go there."

I looked over my shoulder, afraid. I grabbed my still-unopened bag of chips and squeezed, crushing its greasy contents. "Baltimore?" I whispered.

He nodded.

"How do you know? How do you know about Baltimore?"

He reached into his massive backpack and pulled out a photo. It was a five-by-seven print that looked to be a few years old. The corners were bent, and it had more than a few creases. The picture showed a green lawn in some public park on a sunny day. A few people in sweaters and jackets, along with their dogs, dotted the lawn. A dense clump of trees rose up in the background, and some kind of brook or rivulet could be seen on the left side of the image. A footbridge crossed the water.

I stared at him. "You know? You know where she is?"

He didn't hear me. He was lost in the picture.

I reached forward and pointed to the trees. "That's where . . ."

He raised the photo and pointed to a dark spot under the footbridge. "That's where we lost him. *I* lost him."

"Him?"

"My brother."

"Lost him?"

"Missing. Disappeared. Taken, I guess."

"In Baltimore?"

"In Baltimore."

I again pointed at the trees and the dark shadows they created. "There," I said. "That's where we lost her."

He looked at me for the first time since he'd taken out the picture, and, for the first time, he saw the fear and panic on my face.

"My sister. That's the exact spot."

"In Baltimore?"

"Yes. Right there." I banged my finger on the trees.

He turned over the photograph and laid it on the table. He stared at me. My eyes were unblinking. All he could say was, "Your sister?"

"My sister."

"And my brother?"

I reached for the photo and turned it back over, holding it close to my face to inspect the elements. I handed it back to Thomas. "That's it. The same spot."

He placed the photo in his backpack and zipped it shut. Both of us looked down at our trays and could think of nothing better to do than to finish our meals.

LABOR POLICY

I T MAY BE SURPRISING, but our research of court records, which we conducted to discover what impetuses might exist to kidnap children,
indicates that two years ago there were twenty-eight separate cases of
proven human slavery in the city of Baltimore. An assistant at the archive
assured me that close study of social services records would reveal at
least as many more cases that were dismissed or improperly investigated.
He said that half of these questionable cases, most involving the adoption
of adolescent children by distant (and not-so-distant) relatives, could be
revealed as cases of human slavery, but only if social services ignored
the stringent rules set by the city to justify unannounced home visits,
which are time-intensive (and often dangerous) operations. Documented
accounts of neighbors and witnesses detail screaming children kept home
on weekdays, forced to work in what can only be described as suspicious
mail-order businesses. Some suspects are even accused of serially adopt-
ing unwanted children to establish an unpaid labor force. Complaints are
made in many cases, but there must be a certain number lodged to justify
an investigation, and files are closed after time has passed, which, in turn,
returns the complaint count to zero. These files become public record
after several years, but, the court employee noted, they often disappear
mysteriously when new complaints are lodged against a household that
was reported in the past. Officials say this policy is in place as an aus-
terity measure. If they investigated claims of human slavery that were
registered once, twice, or even three times, they would need to hire dozens more investigators, an unthinkable cost. Even though it would most
likely afford more than one hundred city residents their basic human free-
doms, they would surely be angry and emotionally damaged, putting an

incalculable strain on the city's counseling services and penal system. The city council supports this policy and, by necessity, ranks human slavery very low on the list of the city's woes.

PROPER AUTHORITY

A FEW MONTHS AFTER MOVING TO BALTIMORE, we heard of a man named Jason Tucker who was an artist, as was his wife, and, as such, had no health insurance, which proved tragic when she fell ill with an autoimmune deficiency. His wife insisted that Tucker not forsake his sculpture for a day job with benefits, but, while he felt that he ought to grant her this wish, he did attempt to pay the doctor bills by playing poker, as he had always been good at cards and games of chance. He began playing online, but, as medical specialists became involved in his wife's treatment and medical fees rose, it became necessary to play in real games that were held at odd hours in small apartments, in unfamiliar neighborhoods without bus stops, where the stakes were considerably higher than on the internet. When, however, Tucker's wife made a full recovery, poker had already overtaken his passion for sculpture, and he continued to play and win in these backroom games to the point that he was gaining a reputation that he felt necessitated carrying a handgun at all times, a handgun with which he was shot and killed early one morning after a disagreement between two other men at the table he was sitting at, the nature of which not a single witness could recall. His wife, for whom he had become a gambler, and who was still recovering her strength when her husband was killed, soon learned that she was pregnant, and this made her happy, knowing she would not be alone, even though raising a child would be difficult without her husband. The baby was born—it was a girl who took right to her mother's breast but screamed if anyone else came near her, a behavior that persisted after they returned from the hospital. The months passed, and the mother's friends and family stayed away from the baby, afraid of disturbing the fragile peace she found at her mother's side. For several months, the new widow consoled her daughter and forsook the company of others, as it unfailingly angered the infant. One afternoon, the child began to scream uncontrollably, simply because the mail carrier had dropped a note through the slot in the front door, so the mother, feeling the melancholy and isolation had become unbearable, grabbed the baby, who lay in her crib, by the throat and crushed her trachea with a sharp thrust of both thumbs, bringing a quick end to the crying and a slower end to her daughter's life. She immediately picked up the phone and notified the proper authorities. This reminded my companion and me that just as when we were young, the people of Baltimore were quick to squander a child's life.

THE SWIMMERS

M Y NEIGHBOR'S SON was known for swimming great distances, sometimes through treacherous bodies of water, but not as part of organized swim competitions; it was an obsessive personal challenge. When
he saw a broad harbor, a turbulent stream, a chilled creek, he became set
on crossing it. These challenges had always ended successfully, until he
made an error. Having swam the breadth of the Inner Harbor amid boat
traffic and other obstacles, having crossed the Little Falls Branch rapids
just above the Potomac tidal basin a week after spring warmth had melted
a winter's worth of snow, he planned to simply swim a quarter mile downstream in a trickle of rivulet in the city park near our neighborhood, then
swim another quarter mile back upstream. He invited a young boy of ten,
also from the neighborhood, to swim with him, expecting the boy would
reject his challenge as everyone always did, and opt to stand on the bank
and cheer him on. There was a group of spectators gathered, who were all
surprised and excited when the young boy accepted the offer and dove right
into the water, and, with my neighbor's son, the great swimmer, watching nervously from the bank, the boy swam effortlessly downstream until
he was out of sight. The onlookers cheered for the boy and laughed at
the accomplished swimmer standing half naked and dry beside the water.
Without warning, he himself dove into the rivulet and swam after the boy,
who had yet to come back into sight. My neighbor's son understood that
the second upstream leg of the swim was the real challenge. Several minutes later, the young boy did reappear, swimming vigorously, arriving safely
at his destination. But my neighbor's son, the great swimmer, did not
return, because, as the boy explained, he was taken under by the upstream
current and seemed to lack the strength to pull himself up from under

it. The question we cannot answer is why the unproven young boy could successfully swim the same course that took the life of the accomplished swimmer, who had completed several much more difficult challenges. My companion and I can't help but wonder if whatever strange presence that claimed our brother and sister so many years ago in a Baltimore public park also took the daring swimmer for its own.

SATISFACTION

MY YOUNGER COUSIN (on my mother's side), who had dated the same woman for many years and never proposed marriage to her, left her on his thirtieth birthday, only to move in with her mother, from whom she was estranged following her parents' messy divorce. He began to fight with the older woman, and, after three years, left her to return to her daughter—with whom he also fought—until, a year later, he left her to return to her mother, whom he had grown fond of again. Yet, I believe he understands that he will abandon the mother again for her daughter only to come back again for as long as it takes him to truly feel loved by one woman or the other. His own mother, a subway conductor who was my mother's sister, was married to two men two times each, and had a child with each of them (my cousin and his half sister); she eventually found love with another man, whom she met on the subway one day and flew to Miami with the next. They spent three days in a luxury hotel room, ordering steak and champagne and freshly squeezed orange juice from room service, finally emerging only to relax on the beach. This man with whom she had found love reported that my aunt stood up at one point in the lazy afternoon, walked into the surf, and swam gracefully into the waves, never to come back ashore. My cousin and mother hated her for this, claiming she was concerned only with her own contentment and not the well-being of her family. Truthfully, I think what really bothered my mother about her sister's suicide was the reminder that our family members, whether young or old, could disappear at any given moment.

EMPLOYEE OF THE MONTH

A N EMPLOYEE AT THE HAMBURGER RESTAURANT that we visited on nights when we were too tired to cook for ourselves was fired unceremoniously, simply because he had a habit of gulping unusually loudly as he drank water, which was quite often, as the heat of the kitchen made him extraordinarily thirsty. The other line cooks found this habit amusing at first, but, as months wore on, the gulping became unbearable, almost unexplainably unbearable, so much so that they conspired to get their coworker—who was otherwise conscientious and efficient—fired. They created a false security video in which a stand-in for the cook spat into a customer's double-decker cheeseburger. The daytime and weekend managers immediately dismissed the tape's evidence as inconclusive grounds for firing their best cook, but the tired night manager sent him home immediately after viewing the tape. This night manager, I learned from a plaque that appeared on the wall several months later, was named Regional Employee of the Month and praised for encouraging worker morale and increasing efficiency.

4

ORDERED A CHOCOLATE MILKSHAKE. I had almost cleared a plate of American-cheese-smothered fries and he still hadn't arrived. I always felt funny, even as a teenager, sitting in a restaurant sipping only water. I'd been pushing a lawnmower for a landscaper all summer, so, when the sun went down, I had a big appetite on those days when I wasn't sick from sunburn.

I hadn't seen my friend for a week or so. He had been out of town at freshman orientation for the college he'd be attending in the fall. But we had spoken on the phone once during the week. Briefly. He had called from a payphone in the dorm and said something about meeting someone, someone who knew something.

As I got to the bottom of my milkshake, he walked in, accompanied by a young woman. She was tall, with strikingly pink skin that stood out against her black hair. She stood behind him. I thought she was hiding herself.

He smiled and nodded. He pointed to an empty seat in the booth beside me. "Please," he said, motioning to his companion. "This is Barney."

The girl sat lightly, one leg swung to the side. If she needed to make a quick getaway, she could. He sat across from us. "This is Lucia."

I would have offered a hand, but Lucia didn't seem like someone who wanted to be touched, however perfunctorily. I smiled at her, hoping to put her at ease. She gave me a quick wave, but offered no eye contact.

"We met at orientation this weekend," he explained.

Lucia let out a sharp cackle, more gasp than laugh. I was already on edge and slid farther into the depths of the booth. Was this the person he had met? The one who knew something? She brushed her hair away from her face. It was straight and black, just like mine. This frightened me. I was afraid of what my friend was about to tell me.

"I've told Lucia about Baltimore," he said. He smiled at her and she looked at me, studying my face closely. "Apparently, she knows all about it. She's been there."

I looked back at her. For the first time, she smiled.

The waitress came to the table and asked if we wanted anything. "A grilled cheese," he said. "Pickles, lettuce, tomato, fries on the side." Lucia looked at him. "She'll have the same."

I was surprised by their intimacy. "So, you just met this week?"

"Yes." Again, Lucia smiled.

"When Lucia was in Baltimore she lost something too." He slid himself directly across from me. "She lost a brother." He looked from me to Lucia and back again.

"And I've never found him." She looked at me as if I might have a solution for the mystery.

I finished my milkshake.

My friend looked behind the counter. "God, I'm hungry. I didn't even realize. What time is it anyway?"

"10:38," Lucia said.

I whispered across the table, clear enough for Lucia to hear, "Did you tell her? About us? Or what happened to us? To them?"

"Yes. What do you think we're talking about here?"

"But I've stopped looking," she said. "You both spend your lives looking for something that isn't there. I know better."

He shook his head. "This is where our conversation breaks down."

"So why are you talking to us right now?" I asked.

"Exactly," he said. "Why did you even tell me that you lost a brother"— again he looked at my face and hers—"in Baltimore. Why did you show me that article?"

"What article?"

"The one about my mother. A feature story from the local paper back home. About her search for my brother. I gave up. She hadn't. Or hasn't, I should say."

The waitress returned with their orders, placing a grilled cheese in front of each of them. Nobody looked up. Lucia began to eat and I watched her, while my companion watched me watch her.

"So," I asked again, "why are you sitting here with us?"

"I thought I explained," he said. "We met at orientation this week."

I ignored him. "Why did you come all the way here with someone you just met, who happened to lose a brother in the exact same place you lost a sister?"

Lucia dragged a french fry through ketchup and ate it.

"And why are you showing my friend empirical evidence of your missing brother? Why bother proving to someone that you're missing something you don't want to find?"

"I didn't say that I don't want to find him."

"That's true." My friend smiled.

"I just said I'm not looking for him."

"I don't believe you."

"I tend to agree with you." He caught Lucia's eye and she smiled back, shrugging.

I was not smiling. "You expect me to believe that you came here to meet me—me, who lost a sister in Baltimore—and you're not trying to find your missing brother?"

"I don't expect anything of you," she said. "I can't expect anything of you. I don't know you."

I looked away.

"And who said I came here to meet you?"

"I didn't," my friend said. He had finished his french fries and begun to pull Lucia's from across the table.

"So what are we doing here?"

"I'm eating," he said.

"Well, I'm done." I stood up.

My friend looked back and forth between Lucia and me one more time.

"I have to work early tomorrow. Would you mind standing up so I can slide out?" I left a bill on the table.

Lucia stood without looking at me. I slid out and mumbled, "Nice meeting you."

"We'll talk tomorrow," he called after me.

I walked slowly down the wheelchair ramp outside the diner, past the windows separating its booths from the outside world. Most of them were empty, until I came to the profiles of my old friend and his new friend. Without me there, they sat eating their grilled cheeses in silence. I stood and watched—they didn't notice me. On occasion, he looked up and his mouth opened. I thought he wanted to apologize. But she looked down and ate, her face as still as a sunken stone.

These were not satisfied people, even having presented themselves to me and having filled their stomachs with cheese, potatoes, and grease. But it wasn't a frustrating lack of satisfaction; they were searching for wholeness, and that search sustained them. I watched her as she ate and I felt sure that I was right, and that anybody would agree that she had come to meet me, and that she was very much searching for her brother.

TAKEN

WALKING LATE ONE SUMMER MORNING, my companion and I followed a winding and leisurely route, and eventually found ourselves crossing a public park that looked uncannily (although not exactly) similar to the park where, as children, we had each had a sibling abducted. We discussed how that very coincidence was probably what had first brought us together. We talked about how we had been allowed to keep playing, but our respective brother and sister were taken away and never heard from again. What's worse is that my mother never spoke a word about it after that day, and my companion's mother never left her home except at night, after her child was taken from her. As we walked out of the park, we could hear the final shouts of our lost family members, and we were reminded that a park like that was the very place that called us back to Baltimore.

BAD NEWS

OUR NEIGHBOR'S DAUGHTER, while driving to New York City to start her sophomore year of college, stopped at a rest station in New Jersey to buy some frozen yogurt and use the restroom. While there, she glanced at the headlines on the covers of various magazines and newspapers. On the cover of *USA Today*, she saw an article that described a young man from Staten Island who had been shot and killed, a young man who had the same name as her boyfriend, Russell Jameson, who was also from Staten Island, from the very neighborhood where the shooting occurred. She could not believe her boyfriend had been killed, and, moreover, that no one had informed her. Without buying her yogurt, she drove directly to his parents' house on Staten Island and left a quickly scrawled, but emotionally inspired, note of regret and condolence on their stoop when nobody answered the door. She must have been shocked when she arrived at her dorm room to find another note slipped under her door, signed by Russell Jameson. She paused for the first time since she'd looked at the *USA Today* cover, and realized that she may have made a wrong assumption; "Russell" and "Jameson" were common enough names, and there was no picture included with the article to confirm that it was her boyfriend who had, in fact, been killed. She immediately walked to his dorm room to greet him after the long summer apart, but his door was locked, and she thought he must have gone out for dinner. She had no way of knowing that the note left in her room had been dropped there before the summer break (after she had left) and that her original suspicions were correct.

MORAL BALANCE

OUR PARENTS MAY HAVE DONE WELL to learn the lesson that sometimes the best way to protect your children is to create a deep-seated fear inside of them. This was likely understood by a lawyer from Towson, who lived on a particularly quiet block. He beat his neighbor, another man of about the same age, into submission in his own dining room, then bound him to a chair where he kept him for hours, beating him further and mocking him for having urinated on himself. The man's explanation for why he beat this neighbor so mercilessly was that the neighbor had hit his own wife in plain sight of the lawyer's children, who had come over to swim in their in-ground pool. The lawyer entered his neighbor's house that day, claiming he had a real estate investment opportunity he wanted to share, then began to beat him right as they sat down at the dining room table to discuss the matter, two glasses of iced tea set before them. In court, the accused lawyer explained that a week earlier, his children came home with their story about seeing their friends' father strike his wife, and it was then that he'd begun planning to punish the man. His anger must have been substantial, considering that he broke the man's fingers with only his bare hands and beat him badly enough to require sixty-four stitches altogether. Despite the unsympathetic history of the victim, the criminal charges against the lawyer were particularly harsh, because he had, it was revealed, brought his own children with him to witness the violence he committed for several hours against his neighbor. He claimed that he wished to instill in them a sense of "moral balance."

FOREIGN CORRESPONDENCE

F ROM TIME TO TIME, we would host dinner parties, as a way to assimilate with the community, we said, but more likely as relief from the oppressive gravity of our search. One Friday evening, we hosted one such small dinner party for which the guest of honor was a well-traveled journalist, who we hoped would share his stories about the Middle East and the less stable regions of Southeast Asia, areas of the world we knew little of but were concerned about because of the current political unrest. But instead of offering us a chance to learn about the daily life of a postal worker in Jakarta, or the microeconomics of a nomadic Bedouin household, the foreign correspondent took advantage of our captured attention to describe the sexual prowess of various "girlfriends" he had spent time with abroad; they were girls who, as he put it, because of their youth and aspiration to expatriation from the developing world, were more selfless and risky in bed than their American counterparts. The next weekend, our neighbors hosted another dinner party and invited this same journalist, who this time spent the evening praising his own recent series of feature articles elucidating the phenomenon of underage prostitution in the Islamic world. This was a practice he described as more hypocritical and saddening than any other behavior he'd witnessed in his many years as a journalist.

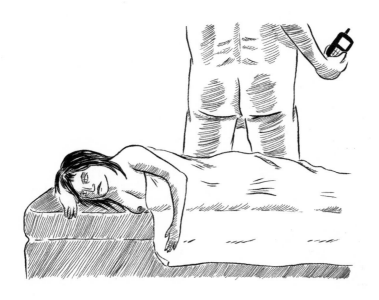

5

AFTER COLLEGE, we spent more time together than we ever had. All three of us. Lucia and my friend moved back to our hometown and shared an apartment, while I lived with my parents, who were only too happy to keep their remaining child close by. After work, my evenings were most often spent in my friends' apartment, eating Lucia's food and watching movies until I fell asleep on their couch. And, of course, we continued our search. We spent hours every night poring over stacks of articles sent to us by microfiche print services, articles we paid for dearly, detailing abductions, disappearances, and even murders of children in Baltimore over the last quarter century. These articles also described the arrests of criminals who we thought would likely be responsible for these crimes. We assembled the documents in webs of logic that physically described the relationships between these people and events, with, of course, the intention of creating some sort of map that might lead us to our brother and sister. We did this while Lucia cooked dinner, a practice that for her was more of a distraction than a passion. As much as our search fueled us, it repulsed her.

She made filet mignons for us one night, with a horseradish sauce, and she begged us to come eat while the food was still warm. We said we would, but thought we had made a *connection*. We sat in the dining room scrawling notes. She called us again and told us if we didn't come eat immediately she would shuffle our stacks of papers into an unrecognizable mess. We looked at each other and laughed, nervously aware that she was speaking in earnest. I followed my fellow investigator into the living room, where three plates sat on the coffee table and the television broadcast a live feed of an early-round men's singles match from Wimbledon. Her food was delicious, but not enough to divert us from the scent we had just picked up. It was a curious news story about a man arrested ten years earlier for a kidnapping he had conducted ten years before that. He had taken a boy from a schoolyard and returned him to that yard a week later, never sexually molesting him or physically harming him in any way. When he was arrested, according to one reporter, he claimed he had done this many times. "Borrowed a child from his parents," he said. We couldn't help but be charmed by his description of his crime. If ever one would have hope for the physical well-being of a long-ago abducted sibling, it would be after hearing a claim such as his. The Baltimore Police Department said his testimony was likely false, as no other similar kidnappings had been reported, and, they asked, who wouldn't report such a crime? My friend and I both agreed that, in all likelihood, neither of us would. Lucia shook her head, put her plate on her lap, and turned toward the tennis match. We also turned toward the match, an awkward gesture of solidarity, and ate the rest of our meal in silence.

We both knew it was best not to return to our research after dinner that night, out of respect for her graciousness and peace of mind. Instead we watched a movie, a comedy about a man-child whose ill-conceived quest for maturity reveals only the merits of childishness. None of us liked the film. Lucia insisted we drink chilled vodka and suck on citrus fruits (limes and oranges) while we watched. The mediocrity of the film and strength of the vodka put us all to sleep before the protagonist got a chance to charm the woman who at first appeared too perfect to acknowledge him.

Lucia woke me up long after the room had gone black. Lying beside me on the floor, she asked, "Who's going to give it up first?"

I blinked and tried to make out the shapes around me. In the grayness of the night, I saw my old friend sleeping on the couch. I looked at her, this woman beside me, a woman I had known for years, but who, in many ways, was still a stranger. "Give it up?"

"Who's going to stop first? You or him?"

"Stop what?"

"The search."

"You know I can't do that."

"Why?"

It was a question I could have answered easily, but I didn't want to hear my answer spoken aloud. My reason for searching was so unjustifiable, so base, I couldn't bear to confront it. It was a compulsion I had no interest in curbing. She turned away, having received the lack of an answer that she had predicted. Feeling the need to fill empty space, I turned her back toward me and kissed her, having no other response prepared. Oddly, she returned my advance even more passionately. She pinned me to the hard wooden floor of their apartment and opened my belt. Without the benefit of even the thinnest sheet, and my friend lying on the couch not three feet away from us, she took off her own pants and got on top of me. We made love slowly and quietly, for what felt like a very long time. The whole time she stayed on top and looked right down at me, but somehow never made eye contact. I was concerned and spent as much time watching my friend sleep on the couch as I did watching her move above me.

When we were done, she lay down beside me and kissed me softly. It was the first tenderness she had ever really shown me. Then she stood up and retired to her bedroom. She didn't come out for the rest of the night.

I looked over at my friend—in the dark, I thought I could detect one open eye. With a groan he turned to face the back of the couch. I couldn't bring myself to get up from that floor and decided to stay where I was and wait for the faint gray light of the earliest sun. I must have fallen asleep at some point, because when the morning came he was gone, and I felt a throbbing ache shooting down the length of my back and neck.

TAKING ADVANTAGE

S OME PEOPLE FALL VICTIM to their own kindness, while some are victimized by the kindness of others. For instance, an autistic man from Greenmount, who spent hours a day at the local convenience store (a store that also acted as a check-cashing business), showed great affection toward the store's owner, Howard Jenkins, who was a well-respected member of the local community. It was known that Jenkins had been robbed at gunpoint on three occasions while delivering money to the bank and had become frightened of this weekly duty. The autistic man, aware of his own superior strength, offered to deliver the money for the man he called Uncle Howard. With earnestness, he said he hated seeing Jenkins scared and would prefer to relieve him of fear. Because the autistic man was found on a Tuesday afternoon (the day Jenkins usually delivered his cash to the bank) beaten to death behind a neighborhood apartment building, many believed that Howard Jenkins, in an act of cowardice, took the autistic man up on his offer to deliver the funds. Jenkins's defenders said those people were needlessly besmirching a good man's name and pointed out that Jenkins never reported a theft that day. Their opponents, in turn, pointed out that Jenkins would be too ashamed to reveal to the police how he allowed his money to be stolen. Everyone with an opinion on the incident was called a liar. The mother of the autistic man said she didn't know who was to blame; she was only sure she had a dead son. (My companion asked if my mother would have preferred to know if her own missing daughter was dead, and I said I was sure she would.)

LABOR AGREEMENT

A T A SUMMER STREET FAIR organized by the local chamber of commerce, we witnessed the president of a major real estate development group, Jim Blackwell, in a serious discussion with Al Horowitz, a successful labor organizer, so we moved closer to the two, expecting to hear some harsh words exchanged, as Blackwell was well known for using nonunion labor. But instead, we witnessed a continuous exchange of back pats and hand-shakes, both verbal and physical. We stood and watched as Horowitz com-plimented Blackwell for his lean and efficient operation, and Blackwell noted the great work Horowitz had done in wresting privilege from the hydra-headed beast of corporate America. Then Blackwell suggested that Horowitz, an avid golfer, join him for a round at the private course of which Blackwell was a member, and, to our surprise, Horowitz said he would be honored. The next morning, as we walked to buy our morning coffee, we watched as the city workers, whose union was in the midst of a bitter dispute with the city government, cleaned up the refuse from the previous day's fair, and we found it to be singularly disappointing when we watched the men sweep away a pile of paper cups left in the exact spot where Black-well and Horowitz had stood and talked.

6

MY COMPANION AND I MET along the parade route late one Saturday morning. He had watched the whole event, the marching bands from local middle schools, the confused Cub Scouts and half-uniformed Brownies, the old men toting the banners of ethno-cultural clubs, and even a group of local adults who were professed "clowning enthusiasts." I arrived shortly after the last float rolled by, and we could just hear the wail of bagpipes approaching the parade's end at the municipal pool. He asked me to walk with him. We could walk straight down the center of the avenue, as the police barricades had been left standing so the street sweepers might come through unobstructed. It was a sunny day. We walked against the usual flow of traffic, stepping on the discarded candy wrappers and cigarette butts the town had left behind.

"I spoke to my mother," he said. This was not an altogether remarkable fact, as he spoke with his mother on most days. "She said my uncle just had his proposal accepted."

"Proposal?"

"For a grant from the federal government to administer medical care in east Africa. In a small town, far from the nearest city."

"That's excellent," I said. "I never knew you had an uncle who's a doctor."

"He's a nurse practitioner, not a doctor, per se."

"Basically the same."

"Basically."

The street sweepers moved by slowly, passing us on either side.

"Right, so he'll be in Africa for a year," he continued. "Essentially running a medication dispensary."

"Can nurse practitioners prescribe medicine?"

"Yes. Or, I believe so. Not sure. Different rules may apply in Africa."

"Could be dangerous."

"What?"

"It could be dangerous to be responsible for a pharmacy in a rural part of the developing world. It's a prime burglary target even here in the U.S."

"That's probably true. I hadn't considered it." He put his arm across my chest and stopped me from stepping in front of an oncoming street sweeper. I had been focusing on the ground instead of looking ahead. "Regardless, my uncle will be moving to Africa, for at least a year."

"Wonderful opportunity."

"For us."

I didn't follow.

"He'll be leaving his home for a year. Which means he'll need someone to watch it for him."

"So this is a house-sitting job? But you have your apartment, and I'm so busy with work . . ."

"My uncle lives in Baltimore," he said, stopping to look at me.

I understood what he was suggesting, and it frightened me. "We're not ready" was all I could say.

"Not ready?" He was angry. "All we do is prepare. All we do is read and research and discuss and study, and as far as I can tell, we still haven't found them."

"I know it seems that way."

"It is that way. If you want to find your sister, and if I'm going to find my brother, we have to go to the place we lost them."

"I know."

"So, I'll tell my uncle he's found his house-sitters."

"I don't know."

He began walking again. I followed, jogging to keep pace with him.

He said, "You've lost focus. Your doubt has nothing to do with finding your sister. It's about *her.*"

"Her who?"

"My roommate. You're afraid she won't follow us to Baltimore."

"I don't know that I would want that for her."

"Well don't worry, my friend. That's the last city she'd ever set foot in."

"And that's why I don't know if it's time."

"Time for what? If you want to find your sister, it's certainly time."

"I agree."

"So," he stopped and grabbed not one, but both of my hands, "what's stopping us then?"

I couldn't respond. If I said her name I thought I would betray the sanctity of our mission.

"It's time we went, and it's time you left her."

"Time I left her?"

"Please, hear me. We can only see a small part of this picture. No matter how much we search, and even if we do find my brother and your sister, the whole picture may never be clear. But there's a reason she hates our search so much. And she is somewhere in this picture that we can't see. She doesn't understand herself. But I do know one thing, and that is that your—" he paused, "closeness will end in nothing but disappointment for both of you."

I wanted to argue; I wanted to fight him right there in the street. But what he said was something that I had understood since the first night she pinned me to that wooden floor. It's probably something I knew since that night we met in the diner, when this strange girl, who had lost someone just like us, traveled all the way to meet me, simply to tell me our search was a mistake.

When we got to the beginning of the parade route, the barriers had been removed and cars had begun to drive down the street. We stepped over to the sidewalk, and she was standing there, expecting us. My friend nodded to her. He knew she would be there. She looked right at him, not even acknowledging me. "Is he going?" she said.

"He is."

She knew about his uncle already and she knew that he wanted to take me with him to Baltimore. I felt as though I had just been administered a test. Only I didn't know whose test it was, and I couldn't begin to fathom whether or not I had passed. Without another word, she began to walk away.

"Wait," I called. "You have to understand."

She stopped and didn't turn. "Are you going to Baltimore?"

"Yes," I said. "But . . ."

"Then you're lost."

She continued walking and I had no right to stop her. Hours later, tired and a little drunk, my friend and I went back to the apartment. She had left. Her room was empty, and the kitchen had been cleaned. She had cleansed and filtered her presence so thoroughly that she left behind not even so much as a ghost.

THE MOST PROFITABLE POETRY READING

A SELF-PROCLAIMED *experimental poet,* who was known for her breadth of knowledge concerning early twentieth-century avant-gardism and her ability to recite the notable sound poems of Hugo Ball, Kurt Schwitters, and F. T. Marinetti at astonishing rates, gave a reading in a crowded local coffee shop and sold more books than she had sold at all of her other readings combined. She was surprised and delighted, especially considering that the reaction of the audience was largely distracted and bored. As the poet was leaving, an employee informed her that they had included a coupon for a week's worth of free coffee with each book purchased, which was an incredible value for regular coffee drinkers, considering the small book of poetry cost only eight dollars.

REGULAR

URING MY FIRST WEEK IN BALTIMORE, at the small café on my corner, I was served by a charming woman, the mother of several children whom she was wholly dedicated to and whom she spoke of freely. She described, among other things, taking them to opening day every year at Camden Yards. Only after ordering coffee and pie each day for a week did she mention that her daughter was in the hospital with a life-threatening illness, but, she said, it relieved her pain to work each day and talk to her customers about their families—and hers. This café became a stop on my daily rounds. I was always sure to sit in her section, and I was always sure to share an anecdote about my family back home. When, six months later, she was absent from work every day for a week, I asked another waitress, a new woman, where she had gone. Her coworker told me that she had taken time off because her daughter had just been admitted to the hospital with a life-threatening illness. I told her she was mistaken; her daughter had been in the hospital for months, and the waitress never missed work, as her job was absolutely necessary to her mental well-being, considering her circumstances. In turn, the new waitress corrected me, informing me that the first daughter had died almost a month previously, and now her younger daughter was in the hospital with the same ailment: pneumonia. Despite our almost daily conversations, the waitress had never even suggested her daughter's death. I stopped buying my coffee at that particular café, and, when I walked by and saw that the original waitress had returned, I always felt a pang of remorse not knowing if she had lost one daughter or two.

THE GOD'S HONEST TRUTH

ON THE CORNER OF THE BLOCK where we lived, right in front of the twenty-four-hour convenience store, a long-bearded man, who was presumably homeless or in some way destitute, sat every morning, always with a new story explaining why he needed money: sometimes for a bus, sometimes to buy the paper to check on his investment portfolio, and, at other times, to pay greens fees at the local golf course. The charm of his ruses made it difficult for anyone not to spare him a dollar or two. He became the subject of a great deal of amused attention one morning when he stood across the street from his usual corner, in front of a gutted townhouse halfway through a complete renovation, and ran back and forth, pointing inside, yelling that a strange woman had just pushed his son down a hole and that he'd never see the boy again, and that the woman was getting away. He said he was telling *the God's honest truth*. He let out a wild laugh and we all laughed in return, surprised to see the man so animated that morning. His performance attracted the attention of the police, who went inside the house to appease him. Inside, they found the body of a young boy who had fallen from at least the third story of the house and had broken his neck on the basement's cement floor. Newspaper reports confirmed that the man, a public school teacher who had been on a medically excused leave of absence for several years, was indeed the boy's father. (The article did not mention the woman who had supposedly pushed the boy, or any foul play at all.)

THE SHUT-IN

IN THE BASEMENT OF AN OLD MANOR in Roland Park, a construction crew that was cleaning out a basement before beginning a massive renovation of the house found, inside a supposedly impregnable safe that they had nonetheless opened, a stooped and frightened man. He ran as soon as they opened the safe's door, fleeing out the front entrance of the house. The workers were too stunned to pursue him, but they all agreed that he was missing fingers on both hands. According to the family who owned the estate, the safe door had not been opened in almost a decade, and there was no other way in or out of it. They also agreed that there were no means of sustenance—including air to breathe—that would allow a man to live inside the sealed cell for ten years. My companion and I wondered if this escaped man might be one of the children, now grown, that we had come to Baltimore to find, but we settled on no resolution concerning this issue, as we argued over the probability of whether it was more likely my sister who was missing or my companion's brother who had been stolen.

HOLIDAY TRAFFIC

WE AVOID THE Fort McHenry Tunnel when driving back into the city after our Memorial Day holiday, as more than half of Baltimore's metro-area residents would pass through the tunnel that day. We wondered how it would affect Baltimore's need for schools if one of the massive freighters navigating into the city's harbor from Kobe, Japan, carrying thousands of sedans to supply Toyota dealerships up and down the eastern seaboard, were to sink right above the tunnel and breach its ceiling on that Monday afternoon.

LIFETIME SUBSCRIPTION

M Y FORMER NEXT-DOOR NEIGHBOR, who ran the local video store and, as such, was known as Movie Man, boarded a train to Montreal on the same day we left home for our yearlong stay in Baltimore. Right before leaving, my neighbor had a phone conversation with a *Daily News* salesman and agreed to buy a lifetime subscription to the paper. Despite planning a long trip, he asked no one to collect his mail and newspapers while he was gone. The Canadian authorities reported that there was no record of him arriving in Montreal or even crossing the border for that matter. He had no family to report his disappearance, but eventually he was listed as an official missing person, although not much of an investigation was conducted, as the detectives had no leads. Meanwhile, his video store was shut down and its entire inventory was auctioned off online by a savvy nephew, who took an interest in his uncle's estate. The profits were used to pay off his outstanding debts, including the lifetime subscription to the *Daily Record*. In time, his house will also be sold at auction and his store will most likely be bought by a proprietor intending a new type of business, surely one that can take advantage of ample display shelving (perhaps a novelty figurine salesman or some sort of a glassware merchant). To this day, whenever I ride the train, I think of how we saw him in the station that day. We were waiting patiently for our later train and he ran frantically past us just as the final boarding announcement was called for the train to Canada. Yet, he still paused to wave to us and wish us luck on our journey. We shared a sympathetic moment, all three of us understanding that we had to leave home that day, and not a day later. He was escaping north (or so he claimed), and we were returning to Baltimore to claim something we had lost. I believe that any success we had during our trip was largely the result of this parting fortune that our former neighbor offered us (probably the last luck he ever offered). On the other hand, to avoid the misfortune that befell the Movie Man on his trip to Montreal, I refuse to sign up for any lifetime (or even long-term) subscriptions, no matter how tempting the offer might be.

7

WE SAT ON THE STOOP of our borrowed home in Baltimore early one evening. We were new to town and there was a lot to learn, so we hoped to encounter our neighbors returning home from work or going out to get something for dinner. We thought we might see children playing on the sidewalk before bedtime. But Baltimore is a strangely quiet city, even during the normal pedestrian rush hours. Some people did walk by, but they were usually alone, always distracted, and certainly did not stop to talk to us.

Still, there was a person, a presence that insisted we heed it. A very old woman sat in a lawn chair on the sidewalk directly across the very narrow street from us. She held a piece of paper that she rubbed between her fingers and she sobbed loudly enough for us to hear. Despite the parked cars between us, her display became impossible to ignore. Of course, my companion approached her before I did. By myself, I would never have acknowledged her crying, because I would have doubted my ability to console her so completely. I watched my friend as he naturally placed his hand on her back. He said something I couldn't hear. She looked up and, although still distressed, I thought she smiled. Then she looked directly at me watching her from across the street, and the fear crept back into her eyes. My friend beckoned me with a slight nod of his head, and I knew it would be wrong not to join them.

I waited for a few cars to pass; I could tell the woman had begun to speak. I approached them. Encountering a crying adult in public turns most polite social protocol on its head. It becomes further complicated when this person is your new neighbor. I thought to offer my hand and my name, but it seemed insensitive. My friend, aware of my ineptness, helped me. "She's lost someone," he said.

"I'm sorry, miss," I fumbled for words. "For your loss."

"A child," he said. "No illness, no accident. He's gone."

She was one of us. I lowered myself before her and held her hand. "I'm sure my friend has told you . . ."

". . . how sorry we are," he interrupted, looking at me with wide eyes that made it clear it was time for me to quiet myself. "Where did you last see him?" he asked.

"Right there." She pointed at our stoop.

"In front of my uncle's house?"

She nodded.

"When was this?"

"Seventeen years ago. Not a week after your uncle moved in. He never told you about this?"

"He may have." And that was the truth. The reason my friend could not remember was not because he was so callous he might have forgotten the story of a child gone missing—we spent most of our days collecting and cataloging such stories—but because stories like this were so frequent in this neighborhood that his uncle was likely to have shared many stories of missing and abducted children that he knew. The woman was probably aware of this, but, of course, one's own tragedy takes a clear precedence over the tragedies of others.

"He had just learned to ride a bike with two wheels. He didn't need someone to hold him. His father let him go up and down the sidewalk. That day we let him cross the street."

"And what happened?" I asked.

"He just rode up and down that side of the street. On that sidewalk right there in front of your uncle's house."

"So how was he lost?"

"His father and I sat right here and watched. The only time we lost sight of him at all was when he went behind a parked car. Not for more than a second. He'd always reappear right away. It's not something you even think about."

My companion placed his hand on her back again. He understood the tragedy that occurs when we assume any outcome is a given.

"One time he didn't reappear. We waited a minute for him to ride back on by. But he didn't. His father walked over to make sure he hadn't fallen. They fall a lot when they first get up on a two-wheeler. He found the bike there, right in front of your house. But the boy, he was gone. Can you believe that?"

"I can," I said, perhaps too quickly.

She looked up and down the empty street. "I guess that's what we've come to expect."

My friend held her arm. He could tell she wanted to stand. She was done crying. She shuffled away and opened the door to the basement apartment beneath the stoop.

"It was nice meeting you," I said.

She looked back, confused, as if she had never seen me until that moment. She adjusted her glasses and squinted, inspecting my face. She cleared her throat and walked back into her home.

We returned to our post on the stoop. I was thinking about dinner while my companion kept his eyes open, ready to meet more neighbors.

"Why didn't you want to tell her?" I asked.

"Tell her what?"

"Why we're here. Why not tell her we lost someone too? She might know something."

"Yes, but what that is we don't know. We don't even know that she lost anyone."

"She just told us she did!"

He looked at me. "Do you know her well enough to believe her?"

"I see no reason not to."

"How about the fact that children have been disappearing from this city for years and years and nobody has been held accountable?"

I shrugged.

"And the stories are so often similar. This person lost a child and that person's child was kidnapped, but no one can ever tell us how it happened. It just happened. There's more for us to know, and these people are obviously not willing to tell us yet."

I couldn't argue with him that day, but still, I couldn't fathom how we might conduct our investigation without a single Baltimorean to rely on. To move forward, we would have to find someone to trust. I soon learned that my companion was unwilling to do that.

SECURITY

I F POLICE OFFICERS continue to emphasize the enforcement of order rather than the preservation of civic comfort, a concept that few of them understand, then we will continue to see them as outsiders and practicing fascists who subjugate, instead of as our servants (as their pithy motto would suggest). After a newly unemployed plumber from Rosedale, who had been arrested for public intoxication, was kept in a holding cell overnight without the benefit of food or a phone call, he asked the officer who released him, "When will I feel safe again?" In reply, the officer, who was handing the man back his shoes and other personal items, said, "Give me a break."

EASY

A T A LOCAL BAPTIST CHURCH, while attending a memorial service for a young cashier who had worked at the convenience store on our corner, with whom we had sat on our front steps one week earlier, and who had told us so much about the neighborhood just south of ours, where he lived, and which we knew next to nothing about, we were more saddened and philosophical than we would be at other ceremonies honoring those whom we knew only casually. We questioned how so many revelations could have been offered to us in just one hour of speaking with a man we had assumed to be uncomplicated and unworldly in his outlook. The young man, who rang up our milk and cigarettes almost every day, was always polite but never outgoing, never interested in conversation, until he stopped in front of our house that day and sat down while he smoked one and then two and then three cigarettes (the last cigarette he would ever smoke, as it turned out). His stories that day offered a different explanation for the pain and anger of his neighbors, an explanation we still honor as the truth, even against the ideas put forth by the pundits and the media. He spoke for an hour describing his neighborhood just south of ours (and implicitly describing the peculiarities of our own immediate streets). Then he looked at his watch and said it was time to go. He stubbed out his last smoke and left us with a nod. Walking home that night, he was shot when he resisted a robber, who stole the forty-three dollars that he had in his wallet. He was found by four children from his neighborhood, and these children, all either ten or eleven years old, carried him two blocks to the emergency room, where he died. One of their mothers spoke at the memorial service, as she had known the man who died, and she told us all that his presence in the neighborhood was a singular one; whenever he walked by, the mood was *easy*.

THE WAREHOUSES OF MOUNT WASHINGTON

O N A WALK THROUGH THE NEIGHBORHOOD of Mount Washington, which we knew was near a river, we decided to leave the road and scamper down a decline, hoping to find water. We did find the water, as well as several inhabited old warehouses. We walked through the open door of one to find a full living room set up below a thirty-foot ceiling; no one was inside, but the TV had been left on and there was the smell of recent cooking coming from the kitchenette set up behind the couch. We inspected several of the other warehouses along the river, and in each we found a similar recently abandoned domestic scene. When we returned to town, we asked one of the local residents about the warehouses, as we were considering purchasing a permanent home in Baltimore, should we not feel ready to return home after a year. He assured us that the warehouses were not for sale. In fact, they had been long out of use, although the authorities tended to look the other way in regards to the homeless population that had moved in. When we asked him where they had all gone when we stopped by, he said he assumed that they had stepped out for their daily group bath in the river.

ROW HOUSE OF ILL REPUTE

A T LUCY'S TAVERN, near the ports, where my companion and I would go to learn about the dockworkers' struggle and to hear the best stories told in the city, a strikingly handsome man arrived who appeared almost mad with anxiety. He stood frozen near the entrance, unsure of whether to sit at a table or the bar. From the look of his shoes and hat, we knew that he, like us, was from out of town. We could not understand why the man, presumably visiting or passing through Baltimore, would visit a bar as unremarkable (at least in the eyes of outsiders) as Lucy's, or how he would even end up in this particular neighborhood. We wanted our questions answered, so we invited him to sit with us and our dock-worker friends and immediately ordered him a glass of whiskey, which he drank without hesitation, obviously appreciative. He remained silent for his first few drinks, but, around midnight, with a few in him, he admit-ted that he was looking for a woman, and that, as he wandered the city, this neighborhood seemed as likely as any to shelter a lonely woman who might appreciate his company. We were in good spirits, and, as such, for our own amusement, sent him to a particular row home not quite three blocks from Lucy's that was well known among locals to be a house of prostitution. The brothel had been there for years, and the same women, who were now well past middle aged, worked the same bedrooms for all those years. We expected that the good-looking man would soon return amused, if slightly embarrassed, after realizing the joke we had played on him. But he never came back. We did see him again two weeks later, sitting on the stoop of the exact house to which we had sent him. He was holding the hand of the woman who was known to be the longest tenured of the women who worked inside the house. The next time we saw him was on an evening news report about his trial for involvement in a prostitution ring, and all the footage showed him standing outside the courthouse, still holding the older woman's hand.

THE FAMOUS SHORTSTOP

THE AWE THAT I FELT for a certain professional shortstop (of whose team I was not even a fan) almost overwhelmed me when I learned that he was sitting not three stools down from me at a bar one night. I nearly spilled my drink when my companion asked the baseball player to sit with us, and he accepted. This moment was a shining example of the admonition that you should never meet your idols if you want them to remain your idols. The shortstop began to drink regularly at this bar, which we frequented, and the more we spoke with him, the less we liked him. We even had to change the channel when his team was featured on *Sunday Night Game of the Week*. He offended us so completely that our stomachs turned when we saw his back at the bar on entering the room. Eventually, we stopped going to that bar—a comfortable place that we enjoyed in every way, except for that one horrible customer—and after that we could never again watch the man play baseball; his fluid, level swing and once-graceful play in the field now seemed awkward and labored. The athlete whom I once respected beyond the usually strict boundaries of team allegiance had ruined that admiration and, with it, my joy in his play, by accepting our invitation to share a drink that one night and by inviting himself to share so many more drinks on so many more nights. If ever we saw his name again in a box score or a highlight of his at-bat on television, my companion and I both covered our mouths, as if the very thought of him might cause us to vomit.

COLD WATER

M Y COMPANION AND I ATE DINNER every Thursday night at the same French restaurant, which is located in the lobby of an austere apartment building in one of the quieter parts of the city. We always enjoyed it, not only for the rich food it served, but also for the lively clientele it attracted. One week, we arrived later than usual and no tables were available in the dining room, but the maître d' did offer us two seats at the bar, which we happily accepted. A group of three women who worked together at the office of a local spice merchant were already sitting at the bar, having finished their dinner, and were enjoying their third bottle of wine. Wary at first, we quickly warmed up to the good-natured trio, and by dessert we were singing along with them, belting out the choruses of their favorite pop songs. As the night wore on, all the diners finished their meals and left, but the bar was kept open for the five of us. We began sharing stories with one another, then one of the women suggested that each of us share our most unsettling memory. While each story was remarkable in its own right, the one that stuck with us, in particular, involved a matter that never came to pass, but that concerned a subject of considerable interest to my companion and me. One of the women, as a girl of seven years old, suffered from typical jealousy toward her toddler brother and, as her mother prepared dinner one evening, carried the young boy out to the river behind her house with the intention of drowning him. If her father had not been returning from his evening walk and had not plucked the boy from the chilly autumn water, her brother would surely be dead and not residing in Denver today. And, she believed that she too would be gone, and not sharing in her fifth bottle of wine in a French restaurant that evening.

89 JOHN DERMOT WOODS

8

ON THOSE EVENINGS when our investigations got us very close, perhaps closer than we really wanted to be, we often had to step out. We would take long walks to distant parts of the city. It was important that the journey was of a remarkable distance and that we both maintained a brisk pace the whole time. We would often begin anxious and distracted by our research, with the hope that our minds would be put to rest by physical exertion, and that by the time we reached our destination, the particulars of which were a minor concern to us, we might think clearly again. At times we went somewhere as obvious as the harbor, and at other times we visited neighborhoods with names we'd never known, somewhere on the other side of downtown. When we'd get to wherever we were going, we'd drink. Usually he would drink beer and I would drink liquor, but that was by no means a rule. There were occasions when we would drink one drink, but those occasions were rare. Often we'd have another. Most often, we'd drink several. And, then, each night ended with a long walk home. This walk was not for exercise but for balance. At the very least, this concluding walk helped ensure that our headaches would lessen in the morning and our bedrooms wouldn't spin around us as we laid our heads to sleep.

One afternoon, we were reading through the original news articles detailing the abduction of a local boy, and realized that we could actually see the back of his parents' home from the rear windows of the house in which we were living. So, my companion and I spent the evening on the back porch observing the quotidian movements of their house, the heads entering and exiting the kitchen, the young woman (the missing boy's sister?) stepping out to smoke a cigarette in the yard. This kind of work was exactly the kind that taxed both our psyches and our consciences. We needed to take a walk.

The walk we took that night began as the simplest of our walks. We went directly to the center of the tourist area and found a chain restaurant with outdoor seating by the water. We paid too much for a couple of drinks and, satisfied, decided to walk back home, no worse for the wear.

As was often the case, though, we stopped for another on the way home. We found a very small and very empty bar in Poppleton. The bartender was quiet and so were we, and we found ourselves in the comfortable rhythm of ordering rounds. Our drinking and walking was doing its trick that night, but still, I was relieved that upon exiting the bathroom, I saw my friend was standing beside the bar door with his coat on. He had taken the initiative to start our walk home. I saw that he had already left a tip on the bar. I thanked our bartender and followed my friend out into what had become a chilly night.

Other than noting the drop in temperature, we said very little to each other as we walked home. On that evening, our shared silence suggested shared contentedness. Despite our drunkenness, our pace was quick and regular, lulling us into a meditative reverie.

This spell was broken when it dawned on me that someone was walking several paces in front of us, and had been for some time. Unintentionally, we had been following this figure. We drew closer and the figure appeared to be that of a young boy, although we couldn't be sure of anything in a night that dark. Closer still, and it appeared the boy was wearing shorts and no coat. He must have been cold in the night's chill, but his deliberate pace suggested he was perfectly comfortable. Stranger yet, his feet were apparently bare, a daring undertaking on the Baltimore streets, no matter the weather. My friend and I looked at each other, confirming that the other had noticed this child. I quickened my pace, to see if the boy needed our help, but my friend stopped me and signaled for me to slow down. He wanted to follow, to observe, as that was, after all, why we had come to Baltimore.

The boy's path led straight back to the neighborhood in which we were living. This was an expected coincidence. He walked down one of the drives that go behind most houses in Baltimore. These lanes are lined with backyards and small driveways, usually patrolled by scores of rats. The boy stopped behind one house and stared up at it. We stood back in the shadows and watched him. Soon, a loud bang came from inside the house, and I thought I saw the boy nod, as if the sound was something he was expecting, perhaps even planning for. The bang could have been the sound of a slammed door as easily as that of a gun.

The boy suddenly swung around and appeared to look straight at us, although it was hard to imagine he would be able to see us in the dark shadows. A moment later, a delivery van turned into the alley, driving as if it was going down an empty boulevard. We pinned ourselves against the fence behind us to avoid getting hit. The van screeched to a halt and we saw the boy's face flooded with the shine of its headlights. I thought he looked particularly unafraid. He stepped to the side. We heard the van door open and close, then it drove off as quickly as it arrived. The boy, of course, was gone.

"Why would they let us see that?" my friend said.

"Who? Who let us see what?"

"The ones who took your sister. And my brother. And the boy across the street and the other down the block and the girl at the middle school and the two friends on the class trip and the infant in the park and all the other children. They wanted us to see that."

I stared at the empty, quiet spot where the boy had just stood. Already I began to question if we had really seen him. It was only my companion's corroboration that made me believe I hadn't wholly invented the incident.

"They want us to know it's not over."

COVERAGE

ONE AFTERNOON, following a long and lazy bus ride to Dundalk (a neighborhood we often visited, as it felt like a place where we were likely to find our missing siblings), my companion and I met a man with nobly graying temples who gave us many more details about Rabbite's final days, those spent in his decrepit row house, than we had gotten from the newspaper account in the *Sun* on the previous Friday. The man had such insight into Rabbite's decline because he volunteered for the local Meals on Wheels program and had delivered Rabbite his lunch every weekday. He was witness to the end of the man we believe was the greatest documentary filmmaker the city has ever known. We met the volunteer in a sign-less pub that we always visited on our bus trips to the southern part of the city, a pub that was usually full of restless men playing only guitar-driven pop songs on the jukebox. It was his gentle demeanor and way of sipping, not gulping, his beer that attracted us to him. We sat down on stools on either side of him and shook his hand, then he told us that for many years he'd been a television news reporter who covered notable house fires for WJZ. Upon first looking at him, we had assumed that he paid his bills as either a gardener or a kindergarten teacher, and we were hoping he would share his ideas concerning simple daily pleasures, not the politics of media, which we had left our neighborhood to forget about. But he didn't burden us with tales of "coverage" or "breaks." He explained that while he had once been the first on the scene at all the city's major fires, he had, in fact, resigned unexpectedly ten years earlier. It was the night following a conflagration that consumed a whole block of homes in Butcher's Hill, the largest fire he had ever reported on, that he committed himself to the city's forgotten. He claimed that he had never second-guessed this choice, and that he absolutely never watched the evening news (unlike Rabbite, he told us, who watched WJZ every night, at both five and six o'clock). He quickly got a gig driving the Meals on Wheels van and the first meal that he delivered was to the great filmmaker, who immediately recognized the deliveryman as the face of Baltimore's many fires. Not only did he bring Rabbite his lunch every day, but he also ran reels of film back and forth across town to help the old man finish the final cut of his last film, *The Tribulations of Vacations and Getaways*. As he traveled to and from the editing lab, he never dared to open the film canisters and hold the master's work before the sun to see what his camera had captured. When Rabbite died, our friend was the first one to see his new corpse. For all the afternoons they spent together, he said, all things considered, he never knew Rabbite, even as he laid his small body on the white sheets of his familiar twin bed.

OBSCENITY TRIAL

A CARTOONIST WHO HAD CREATED HIS OWN COMIC BOOK was brought to court, accused of obscenity by an unsuspecting reader who bought the book at Planet Hero, which the cartoonist referred to—even on the stand—as a local *smut shop* run by a *smut peddler* who never thought about the content of the merchandise he sold and how these books might weaken their readers. Professionally, the cartoonist explained, he had only been successful by creating covers by which his books could not be judged. Comic book readers wanted their existing inclinations served and were unlikely to pay money to be unsettled or made uncomfortable. Many years ago, he decided to draw a well-muscled and shirtless man on one of his covers, and that book outsold all of his others combined. Since that time, his covers have consisted of assemblages of scantily clad women and other stereotypes that in no way relate to the complicated content within the book, and, in that time, his sales have consistently increased from book to book. He claimed that the reader who accused him of obscenity was as ignorant as just about any buyer of comic books, and, accepting this explanation, the judge dismissed the case. When interviewed about the proceedings, the cartoonist said he was quite pleased with the judge's efficiency, and he attributed it to the judge's obvious distaste for the whole medium of comics and those who would spend money on them, an attitude the cartoonist understood well, as he too held the same feelings for his readers and those like them.

97 JOHN DERMOT WOODS

LAST CHANCE

WE WERE ALL DEVASTATED when we learned that the local florist, a friendly and accommodating man who had lived in the neighborhood since long before any of us had arrived, was guilty of rape. Not only was the man (who was in his shop from ten to six every Monday through Saturday) well known to us, but his wife and teenage son were too, as they both worked in the shop and were as open and polite as the florist himself. He had been named Merchant of the Year at least five times and even sponsored the local Pee Wee football team, and, when possible, attended their games. His victim was a young woman who lived two blocks from the shop in a small studio apartment. He claimed they had conducted an affair for over a year, that she had been a regular customer of his for more than a year before that, and that on the day of his crime, she had told him an illicit affair was no longer tolerable, and that it was over. In response, he ended up forcing himself on her, which he fully admitted was because he feared he would never have another chance to be with her again.

SAINTHOOD

WE SOMETIMES VISITED THE COURTS DOWNTOWN to pore over documents that had lain untouched for at least two decades. These courts are a place where professional ambition and a distrust for altruists and altruism run rampant, and which can honestly be called a place where generosity and forethought go to die, and where many more spirited young lawyers are corrupted than fostered into productive careers of service. A middle-aged lawyer was found dead in a men's restroom, having killed himself with an overdose of prescription medications. An e-mail sent to his colleagues one hour previously clearly explained his reason for suicide. It was a long message that began by explaining in detail the bureaucratic wrangling he had endured to set up his free legal clinic. While the clinic was built and now ran successfully, he lost his passion and interest for the work because his energy had been expended on convincing his peers that his goals were both realistic and worthwhile. The eventual apology and praise he had hoped his cynical colleagues would offer when the clinic was opened were never given. He sent letters, arranged fundraisers, issued calls for volunteers, but no one from the legal community responded. It was not the skepticism or ignorance of the other lawyers that drove him to his death; it was the complete lack of hopelessness in their nonexistent gestures. He did not want them to spoil his life's work, so, before going to court that morning, under the cover of darkness, he set the legal clinic on fire. It was reduced to cinders within hours. If they ignored him while he lived, he felt only greater regret that they might admire him after he was gone, when he could enjoy it in no way, and, in fact, his clinic was a greater asset to the city of Baltimore than any of the other lawyers' penny jockeying. The legal system, he asserted in his final e-mail, succeeded only because of the work of living saints who were not allowed full and productive careers, and he had no desire to be canonized and added to a growing list of noble failures.

AN UNEXPECTED WHIM

AN UNLICENSED SUICIDE HOTLINE OPERATOR was charged with reckless endangerment. She was accused of encouraging our neighbor, a distraught man, to shoot himself, based on the fact that she hung up on him the moment before he pulled the trigger of his gun. This was only after she had counseled him and encouraged him to live for several hours. In court, the operator explained that she had been seized by *an unexpected whim*, and that she no longer believed in the glimpses of hope she had offered the man. Furthermore, she felt it was her responsibility, at that moment, to share with him what she thought was the truth, to validate his desperation. She then felt that continuing to coerce the man from his will would taint the truth that she had spoken, so she hung up. A moment later, the man (a divorced attorney) pulled the trigger of his pistol, held at such an angle so as to destroy his brain and the back of his skull. The other hotline operators who sat in the call center that afternoon testified that their unlicensed colleague simply set the phone down and walked out of the center without saying a word. The members of the jury all agreed the operator's decision was reprehensible and surely contributed to the man's death. Yet, when asked by the judge, their foreman pronounced a decision of not guilty. They couldn't find a way to understand her moral reprehensibility as criminal. The hotline the operator worked for had the highest success rate in the city for aiding callers, despite its dubious licensing and hiring practices.

103 JOHN DERMOT WOODS

9

OUR ACQUIRED HABIT of spending afternoons in the public galleries of Baltimore's various criminal courts was my idea. I reasoned that because these abductions had been conducted over the course of so many years, and because the reach of their effects throughout the city was so pervasive, despite so little acknowledgment of their occurrence in any public forum (official or informal), there must be some systemic condition that ensured these crimes continued. The one place where I thought the marginalized were offered a view into the system, at least ostensibly, was the public forum of the courtroom. I was prepared to be disappointed in my assumption, and of course I was, in the conventional way: the cases themselves offered further proof of obfuscation on the part of those with influence. But I discovered the possibility of truths on the peripheries of the courtroom, slightly to the side of the thing in focus. I became enthralled by the lawyers worrying about their wives back home while their clients were pronounced guilty of felonies, and the fathers watching alongside me in the gallery, praying their sons might spend less time in jail than they did, and the aunts who wished for guilty sentences for the nephews afraid of where their lives outside might lead them, and the jury members, who so often fought sleepiness more than bias, and, eventually, my fellow observers in the gallery, many of whom attended the trials every day like me, with the dedication of a daily communicant to mass.

After a few weeks of this routine, my companion began to join me on my trips around the city. While not as enthralled as I was, he thought we might locate some pattern in the cases, in the judges who tried them, in the lawyers who argued them, in the defendants and the crimes they were accused of. He brought a notebook, and his approach to the courtroom had the intensity of a student in the weeks before finals. He believed a code might be revealed to us, and that he might be able to crack it. Of course, his method quickly led to disappointment—if we were going to get answers, they certainly wouldn't reveal themselves in such an obvious way, just as the newspapers and eyewitness interviews did little to help us. His patience was tested by our long afternoons spent simply watching, and he began to accompany me less often.

One day we observed a young man on trial for aggravated assault and burglary. My companion was obviously bored by the proceedings, and it shames me to consider it, but I too had trouble taking interest, because these cases were so commonplace in the Baltimore courts. The defendant, a kid from southwest Baltimore, was a minor being tried as an adult, a typical situation in this particular system. What grabbed my interest was how much like a sixteen-year-old boy he looked. It wasn't the softness of his face or bright eyes, it was the movement of his neck and especially his shoulders. It was the way he turned when the officers of the court addressed him. And it was the lack of either bravado or practiced jadedness in his stammered comments and responses. Moreover, it was his mother, a young woman herself, whom I quickly identified sitting not two rows before me. She watched the proceedings with trepidation, not expectation, naïve enough to believe the conclusion was not foregone. He was being sentenced on that day, and her face showed that she still believed there was a chance of reprieve, or at least a sentence that did not include imprisonment. As he was sentenced to years in jail, her faced crashed more violently than anyone else's. His own simply seemed bewildered. The lawyers spoke to each other and the client respectfully but with urgency. Clearly they would be able to worry about what they were having for dinner that night.

My friend stood up and tapped my shoulder. "Let's go," he said. "It's over."

But the part I was interested in had just begun. "I want to watch."

"We watched. We watched the whole show. Problem, resolution, and so on. Time to move on to the next."

He didn't understand why I spent every afternoon in the courtroom. I wasn't prepared to explain. "Why don't you head out? I'll be with you in a moment."

He walked to the back of the room. He paused and pulled out his notebook, marked something with a pencil, and slapped the book shut before leaving. He might as well have been whistling to himself. He'd placed another mark in his register, another piece of the ever-growing puzzle that he fully expected to complete one day.

I turned back to the boy and his mother, a place where true revelation might exist. They were both talking to a lawyer, a tired man in a gray suit. The lawyer seemed patient as he presumably explained to them the course of the next several years of the boy's life. The child stared right through his counsel, knowing he would soon understand more than anyone else in the room. The mother nodded emphatically in response to everything the man said, fully expecting that answers could be found in his words. I stayed in my seat as the courtroom emptied. I would wait for the next group to file in and observe another trial. I would let my restless friend ride the bus home alone that day.

GUILT

THE AUTUMN MY COMPANION AND I arrived in Baltimore, we attended the public trial of a man from Dundalk who was accused of killing his aging mother. The man, a dedicated member of the carpenters' union and a well-respected foreman for some fifteen years, said he had shot his mother that winter afternoon to alleviate his overwhelming sense of guilt. The jury was confused by this claim, as the carpenter, who many years before was an all-city long-stick lacrosse midfielder, had lived with his mother his whole adult life, providing for her and even driving her to the senior center every weekday. We sat in the courtroom and watched his face contort, attempting to explain his guilt, but he emitted nothing more than a muffled cough, a gesture of inexpression my companion claimed to understand, an utterance that could only have been produced from watching a lifetime of disappointed parents. Character witnesses agreed that, until that winter afternoon, he was the paradigm of filial piety. He had shot her in the base of her skull with a Smith & Wesson .357 revolver, which had lain dormant for more than ten years in a box of his deceased father's cherished possessions. One neighbor testified that he had seen the gun several years earlier, but the carpenter had assured him the firing mechanism had long been disabled, as neither he nor his father had any interest in shooting things.

EASY

A CIVIL ENGINEER whose job was to correctly time traffic lights, particularly in high-volume areas such as those roads near the train station, was tried for the murder of his twelve-year-old niece, whom he had always claimed was his favorite. In court, he could offer no explanation for why he had strangled the girl, but he assured the judge and jury that he did it with the greatest of ease. When the prosecutor pressed the issue, the engineer remained placid and simply insisted that he had committed the act without hesitation or compunction. The jury had no choice but to declare him innocent due to insanity. After reading an account of the trial in the newspaper, my companion suggested that we find the civil engineer ourselves and question him about his involvement in our own siblings' disappearances. When I pointed out that the engineer would have been a child himself at the time we lost them, my companion conceded that he was unlikely to be the guilty party, and that he was lucky not to have been taken himself.

THE OTHER SIDE OF THE FENCE

A PARTICULAR DISTRICT COURT JUDGE was not only respected for his fairness but also admired for his ability and, as such, was invited every year to judge a certain citywide crab cake competition. During the year we lived in Baltimore, while judging the competition, the judge began chatting with a fisherman between rounds, and he realized that crabbing was a fascinating activity that he knew next to nothing about, and so he asked the fisherman to take him out on his boat one day. When the day to go out on the water came, the judge was extremely satisfied; in fact, he was thrilled, as the weather was bracing, the company quiet but life affirming, and the work satisfactorily tiring. At the end of the day, he couldn't help but invite his fisherman host for a beer. As they each sipped from a can of Natty Boh, after the judge had offered the fisherman the most sincere thanks he had ever offered anyone, he told his new friend that he would happily switch roles with him. Without hesitating, the fisherman agreed and insisted that they do just that. He left the bar with judge's robes under his arm and the judge had the keys to the fisherman's boat in his pocket. When the men reported to work the next morning, in effect, they both ceased to exist, functioning neither in their old roles nor able to draw an identity from the new ones they had assumed.

STATUTE OF LIMITATIONS

During the unrest in the early seventies that led to the devastation of Baltimore's industry and commerce, two union leaders who were accused of committing violent acts against the management of a particular plastics manufacturer hid in the basement of a sympathetic friend's Hampden row house. The men were later arrested, but charges against them were dropped when evidence revealed that executives had lied about the physical attack in an attempt to frame their political rivals. After the men left his cellar, the homeowner who had harbored them boarded it up as a way of putting this difficult period in both his and the city's history behind him. Then, recently, a friend of ours bought that very row house from the man's son, and immediately reopened the cellar, which had been closed for many years, hoping to finish the space to create a sort of multiuse workspace and guest room. He made an alarming discovery: sitting in the middle of the dry cellar floor, covered with dust but otherwise undisturbed, was a box of documents and photographs left behind by the two former fugitives. The papers offered detailed personal information about the plastics executives' families, including the schools their children attended and clear, candid snapshots (each neatly labeled) of each of their family members. Our friend brought these items to the authorities, as he felt this evidence suggested that the acquitted men had indeed planned something more despicable and, if they were not arrested when they were, may have kidnapped or done something worse to the plastics executives' wives and children. The union leaders were both alive and in their eighties. One still lived in Baltimore, while the other had retired to South Carolina. Three of the plastics executives were also alive, and they made it clear that they still bore a great deal of anger toward the men they had tried to frame.

The question the authorities are still facing is whether it is necessary or even proper to pursue the decades-old evidence that fell into their laps with the goal of punishing and prosecuting two elderly men. The question my companion and I wrestled with was, what if some other basement in the city contained evidence as to the whereabouts of our missing brother and sister, or our brother and sister themselves?

FORGOTTEN APPOINTMENT

THE BEST PLACE TO ENCOUNTER NEW FRIENDS is out on the plazas down near City Hall, especially in the middle of a weekday, and so, during my time in Baltimore, when the weather was warm, I was sure to eat my lunch there three or four times a week, often without my companion. One afternoon, after I had finished my roast beef sandwich and was preparing to leave, a young woman, not older than twenty-one, sat down beside me, her body slumping, belying some defeat. She startled me, as I thought I saw my sister's face grown into her own, but I reasoned that if my sister was still alive and in Baltimore, she'd be a few years older than this young woman. She said she had taken the subway that morning to the city's west side, where she was going to catch a ride with a friend who was leaving on a trip down south. She appreciated when others found her actions difficult to explain, and this is why she rode the Baltimore subway whenever she could. Most people, especially those living in Baltimore, doubt that the subway exists, but, she claimed, for certain locations, it was certainly the most efficient way to travel. While I had never ridden the Baltimore subway, I understood her argument, as I too found subways the most pleasant way to travel when the stops were convenient. The young woman spoke in a deep slang that broke at times to suggest an advanced education, a ruptured way of speaking that I found comforting. That morning, though, when she got on the subway, she forgot why, as she rode it so often, and simply stayed on until the end of the line. Once there, she got on another train and returned to where she had originally boarded, not far from where we then sat. She had spent the afternoon pacing the plazas, neither eating nor sitting, irritated by the blank space in her memory, trying to recall why she had boarded the train that morning. Just before she sat down beside me, she had remembered her friend on the west side, who had offered her a ride down south to Durham, North Carolina, where the young woman's mother lay sick, with no more than a day or two to live. At that moment, I wished that I hadn't finished my lunch, that I had something—a cold drink, a few grapes—to offer the sad young woman.

A BLESSING

WHEN CORPORATE INTERESTS OWN all the commercial real estate in a particular neighborhood while raising rents and welcoming chain franchises for many years (which cannibalizes local income streams and the neighborhood's unique character), there are a surprising number of residents who are shocked when, on occasion, the shops are vandalized, even looted and burned, in an attempt to drive out those who own them. "I call that a blessing," said a friend of mine who had just left such a neighborhood, a neighborhood in which the last chain restaurant had shut down after the latest incident of civil unrest. Not a week after he said this, my friend moved back home, hoping to help rebuild the community in its own image. Instead, he was killed in a shop fire (the cause of which was never identified) at the local convenience store, where he was buying milk for his morning coffee, a tragedy that occurred even though all outside financial interests had been driven from the surrounding blocks.

MERCY FOR THE STATE

O N THE PLAZA, IN FRONT OF CITY HALL, where the television cameras often gathered, my companion and I noticed a woman sitting on a bench. A stream of visitors approached her, paused to inspect her face, then moved on. In return, she offered little more than a nod. No fewer than four times, a man on a bicycle pulled up and handed her what looked like a stack of magazines and newsletters. As quickly as he arrived, he pedaled off again. It was as if she had her own messenger. The woman wore a sweater and several thick wool scarves, despite the recent mild turn in the weather. Her manner was tired, but her face was young. Sometimes she would smile at a person scurrying across the plaza. (We even wondered if she might be smiling at us, once or twice.) We imagined that she was a recent product of an old Maryland family whose American roots dated back to the state's origin as a Roman Catholic refuge. We imagined that while her father and older brothers shuffled shares of family wealth between investment funds, a secure trust had been put aside to care for the mysteriously damaged apple of their collective eye. My companion and I fantasized about her powers as an idiot savant, or, perhaps more accurately put, as a damaged sage. We pretended that once we had the nerve to approach her on her bench, she would share with us the whereabouts of our brother and sister. We soon learned from a friend at the chamber of commerce that the young woman was, in fact, descended from a colonial family, a family that was substantially and wisely invested in the stock market, but it was the woman herself who managed the fortune. We also learned that she was completely blind and every day walked alone from her row house, almost a mile away from city hall, simply to escape the staff of attendants her father and brothers insisted on employing to cater to her daily needs, who even followed her into the bathroom, both when she washed and when she relieved herself. She always sat on the same bench, and periodic investment reports (in Braille) were brought to her throughout the day. The city owed her a debt of gratitude for personally funding a midtown arts improvement district, which was particularly generous of her considering the fact that her blindness was a direct result of burns she received when a bank of fireworks mislaunched during the grand finale of a particularly wonderful display put on by the famous Grucci family to celebrate Baltimore's first City Arts Festival almost three decades earlier, when the woman was still a young girl. Because of her family's preeminent position in Baltimore's social pecking order, they had been given special seating during the display, which had offered them an intimate view of the Gruccis at work. All those we met in Baltimore agreed that this incident, in which an errant Roman candle both burned and mauled her eye, ruined not only the woman's life, but also destroyed the legacy of those who were once considered America's most respected family of pyrotechnicians (as opposed to the tragic explosion in 1983 that killed two Grucci family members, an incident more commonly cited).

FACTORY RENAISSANCE

IN THE EARLY EIGHTIES, in an old bread factory in Greenmount, a local real estate developer built a video arcade for his daughter, who was two months away from earning her MBA. The arcade, when fully established, would have touted the most game consoles of any such establishment, not just in Baltimore, but on the whole Eastern seaboard. It would have offered visitors 376 coin-operated machines, arranged on three floors plus a mezzanine level—all to be built in a matter of months. Before the game consoles were installed, the infrastructure for a full entertainment complex had to be constructed, including handicapped-accessible restrooms and a full snack bar in which popcorn, hot dogs, and pizza could be prepared. All of this was built inside a factory the real estate developer discovered late one night after taking clients from Miami out to dinner and drinks, when they were lured to it by the smell of fresh bread, a few loaves of which the men loading the delivery trucks were willing to share with the men in suits. Nine separate unions were engaged in the project at one time, which was necessary to convert the bread factory into an arcade in such a brief period. In the week leading up to the arcade's opening, the real estate developer's daughter was arrested on murder charges, accused of killing another woman in her business school class. It was a well-publicized trial that resulted in a guilty verdict and a lifetime prison sentence for the developer's daughter. While his daughter was being tried, the developer decided to stall the arcade's grand opening, and once the verdict was passed down, he abandoned the project altogether, paying the contractors' bills in full and shutting the arcade to the outside world. He had the old bread factory locked up tight with 376 unplugged and unplayed arcade games sitting inside it. When I was in Baltimore, a friend of mine, a commercial real estate agent, acquired the keys to the long-dormant factory and took me inside. The expanse and desolation was astounding for a closed and contained space. The snack bar sat quiet and untouched on the mezzanine and, apparently, most of the arcade games had been sold, although the Ms. Pac-Man terminal remained and was plugged in, whirring and singing softly in a corner lit by its own screen.

10

THE LAST TIME MY COMPANION AGREED to come with me to the courthouse, we saw the blind woman we had observed many times. We had never seen her in the courts before, but it didn't surprise us, as she seemed to gravitate toward municipal facilities. We knew many things about her but had never talked to her ourselves. She got on the elevator with us, and I could sense my friend was excited by her proximity. She was the kind of woman who might know something. But how does one ask?

When we reached the ground floor, I said to her, "After you," and we followed her into the building's lobby. When we reached the front doors, I once again said, "After you" and held the door open for her.

She thanked me, then paused. "You come here often, don't you?"

She'd caught me unaware. I had never seen her there before. "I do. Yes. How do you know?"

"Because I've heard your voice."

I couldn't imagine where. "I do come here often, but not in any official capacity. I'm more of an observer. So I really don't say much when I'm here."

"I don't need much to recognize a voice," she said. "I can hear someone order a cup of coffee or greet someone in a hallway, and that's a voice I can recognize again."

"We've seen you before too," my friend joined in. "But never here. We've seen you around city hall. On the plaza."

"I spend a lot of time there."

"So why do you visit the courts?" I asked.

"Different reasons. Many times it's to check on a financial matter; I run a family business. But often I'm here to watch. It's my way of understanding. I'm sure that's why you're here too."

"I think that's accurate," I said. "I'm not sure about understanding. I think I've given up on that. But at least knowing something more completely than I already do."

"And what is it that you want to know?"

I hesitated to say it aloud, as my companion had taught me to keep our search close to the vest. But he volunteered our exact intentions. "We're hoping to find a sister and a brother we lost many years ago."

"You're not the first," she said.

"And can we assume you come here for the same reason?" he said.

"It wouldn't be the worst assumption. And once it may have been accurate. But now, it certainly is not the reason. Now I am trying to understand systems and their effects. If I know the effect of a system, then I know how to invest in it. It's a form of market research, really."

My friend was persistent. I knew him well enough to tell he put a great deal of importance in this encounter. His instinct told him that this woman was the rare figure who might bring us closer. "So why aren't you searching anymore? Did you find the person you lost?"

She smiled. "You've got the paradigm wrong. What you just suggested is impossible. That's what you need to learn. Once people are lost, they cease to be the people they once were. You might find someone one day, and you might not, but you can't expect that to be the brother or the sister you lost."

"So did you find someone? Someone who was once the person you lost?"

"I discovered something while I sat in these courtrooms, and asked favors of friends in police stations and government offices. I discovered that the tragedy of losing someone is pursuing a misunderstood search and losing yourself chasing something that does not and cannot exist."

My friend shook his head. "You must know something. You obviously know people. And you obviously understand that there is something going on here, a pattern of tragedy. We all know that. But you know why. Tell us why."

"I do know something and I just told you. This pattern, as you put it, is a perfect trap. A perfect trap in which to lose yourself. The more you search for people you've lost—people, I suspect, you know in no way anymore—the more you've been defeated."

My friend was clearly angry. He thought this woman could solve our problem but willfully let it persist. I could see he was about to argue with her. I stepped in. "So, miss, if you're able to, please tell us what we should do."

"Stop," she said. "Just stop. Stop spending days in a courtroom you haven't been summoned to. Stop killing the connections with humans you actually know and can dependably access. Participate in your everyday lives." She paused. "Go home. It's time for you to go home." With that, she walked away. It seemed as if she could bear us no longer, that our ignorance was an affront.

In the weeks that followed, my friend redoubled his search, convinced that the woman's admonitions were proof we were getting close. Her words were a sign that someone wanted us to stop; I couldn't help but take them in earnest. In those unprotected hours, perhaps when I woke in the middle of the night and could not fall back asleep, I found it hard to refute anything she said. But the compulsion I had felt since childhood, the drive my friend and I had nursed and refined over so many years, was too strong to resist. I knew she was right, but I could not go home.

FUDDERMAN'S FOLLY

FRANK FUDDERMAN, with whom we had dinner on Tuesday nights (and, more often than not, played cards with) when we lived in Baltimore, said he had responded to an online personal ad and agreed to meet the woman, whom he had never seen, in front of the Washington Monument in Mount Vernon. The appearance of the woman, when she arrived, did not so much disappoint him as confuse him; he had had a very different and very exact expectation in his mind. When I reminded Fudderman that there is no way to predict such things, and that our powers of imagination will always fail in the harsh light of reality, he quietly folded his napkin, stood up, walked out of our kitchen, and then the front door. After that, no one I knew ever heard a word from Fudderman again. I have to believe that whatever tragedy or fortune has befallen him since that night could not have been inspired by the existential enormity of my offhand comment, as philosophy rarely, if ever, influences human behavior.

ON THE THIRD FLOOR OF UNION
MEMORIAL HOSPITAL

WHILE RECOVERING from a stress-induced case of shingles, I stayed for almost a week in Union Memorial Hospital—a hospital I chose because *U.S. News & World Report* ranked its facilities above all others in the area (and because I needed some sort of vacation, a time away from my companion as our failing mission in Baltimore dragged on, during which I could be waited on and served). An older man named Nathaniel Herman, my roommate, explained that he had once been a middle school chemistry teacher in the neighborhood where I was living at the time, and had been fired because of an unsubstantiated allegation of molestation by one of his female students (though he was offered another job after the court found him innocent). He related to me the exact stories he was told each evening during phone calls he received from a man who claimed to have been one of his students, and who was in the same class as the sexual abuse accuser. During one phone call, the younger man recalled a story that had occurred shortly after Mr. Herman was dismissed: this student wished to contact his estranged teacher, and so he went to all the offices that might have Mr. Herman's contact information, including the offices of the principal, the school board, and the superintendent, all of whom said that the information was confidential, except for one secretary, who furtively scrawled an address on a Post-It note and gave it to the student. The boy said he ran to the house, hoping to see his disgraced teacher. He arrived there to find no one home. He saw no signs of life, just a dead family of raccoons on the living room floor. My roommate, Mr. Herman, thought this was strange, because he still lived in that house to that day (he confirmed the address with his former student), and, as he always did, Mr. Herman asked me what the scene that the boy had witnessed might mean.

EXTENDED SENTENCE

THE PENAL SYSTEM can often provide relief, rather than imposition, for particular citizens. For instance, a homeless man who had already been arrested by the police twice that month, described by one arresting officer as a dangerous indigent just waiting to get cuffed for a violent felony, was picked up again—this time for stealing a small carton of orange juice and three boxes of Honey Bunches of Oats (but no milk) from a supermarket. He was also charged with assault, as he had slapped a cashier across the face when she tried to block his exit with the stolen goods. The man was confused when he was told by a police officer minutes later that he was being arrested for stealing cereal, as he claimed that his gluten allergy made it impossible to eat anything with wheat. Medical records confirmed that he did have a gluten allergy, but surveillance video bore testament to the fact that he nevertheless attempted to steal three boxes of cereal. The police considered letting the confused man go until he slapped the officer across his face, just as he had the cashier. He said that he appreciated an occasional incarceration—if brief—as things on the street were not as simple as they once were.

HOLIDAY PARTY

A S CHRISTMAS APPROACHED during our year in Baltimore, our neighbor said she hoped it wouldn't be as horrifying as last year's holiday, when a particular party ended in tragedy. Apparently, the aging daughter of one of the oldest and richest families in Baltimore had spent most of her adult life as a total recluse, but decided that particular Christmas Eve she would host a gala celebration at the family estate. The night would include cocktails, a seven-course dinner, and dancing to music performed by a chamber group made up of members of the Peabody Concert Orchestra. Whether it was due to anxiety or a desire for control, the hostess positioned herself on a balcony above the drawing room and watched the party from there for almost one hour before entering. When she did come down, she revealed a stun gun, which she used to shock any partygoers who, in her estimation, were either boring, haughty, or sullen. Unlike a normal stun gun, it was later revealed that hers had been modified to deliver a lethal shock. When midnight came and the holiday party was over, the only guests remaining were those whom she had shocked, and therefore lay dead on the ballroom floor or upright at the dining table. Perhaps the most unsettling, yet impressive, reality of the evening was the fact that the chamber group and the waitstaff refused to allow the misfortune to distract them and remained dedicated to their duties, playing every piece until the last and serving every single one of the seven delicious courses.

11

M Y FRIEND KNEW I had lost the trail. Baltimore and that blind woman had unsettled me. He was diligent in his work, but he needed me to keep going. One Saturday morning, he suggested we go to the park. I thought he was talking about the small lawn with benches right in our neighborhood. Then I saw that he was looking at a photograph, the same photograph he had carried with him most of his life, the one that showed the place where our brother and sister had disappeared. That was the park he wanted to visit. We hadn't been there since coming to Baltimore. I believe he thought it was too risky. He was always aware of people, people we didn't know, who might want to end our search. I was afraid of something else. It may have been that I was afraid that our search would end before I was ready for it. Going to that park made me nervous; we could find answers that we didn't want. At least not yet.

Still, my days in Baltimore, and the words of that blind woman near the courts, had unsettled me so completely that my search in the past few weeks had become a dying beast. It was a deer limping through the woods, haunches full of shotgun debris and a broken leg, that kept going because its heart was still beating and its instincts told it to keep going. My search needed new life, and my friend knew it, and visiting the exact place where this began appeared to be the only alternative I had to abandoning the search altogether.

We rode the bus across town, and, strangely, neither of us revealed our anxiety. My companion was relieved, and I was mostly numb. We got off the bus and walked the two blocks to the park. It was a nice park, a bit cleaner than most in Baltimore. It was more active and less lonely than most too. Several groups of friends ate food and lay on the grass. Children chased balls and a few dogs slept beside their owners.

We headed straight for the footbridge—it looked unchanged from the one in the picture, the bridge of two decades past. Beneath it we found the exact spot where his brother was lost. (There were plenty of bridges in Baltimore, under which someone, especially a child, could easily go missing.) The underside of this bridge was a place to take naps, not commit heinous acts. It was shady, the grass was mossy and soft, and a small stream ran by, creating an echo on the bridge's bottom side that encouraged you to close your eyes and sleep. My friend looked at where the water was coming from and going to. He touched the ground lightly and nodded. Then he walked on, and I followed.

We went up a hill to where the park's grass faded into its wooded edge: the exact place that had claimed my sister. I had looked at it in the photo for so long that witnessing its physical reality was almost unremarkable. That is until I saw a girl among the trees, one whom I could barely distinguish from the shadows. This was something I had never seen in my friend's photo. I looked to him to see if he had registered this figure. He was now ahead of me, walking quickly toward her. As we got closer, the figure aged; I soon saw that it was a young woman, a familiar one. She lowered herself into the grass and I quickened my pace. I did not want to lose her.

We finally reached the spot, and there, lying among rich, decomposing leaves and moss, was Lucia, our friend whom we had lost along the way. I called her name, more relieved—relieved that she was here, relieved that she wasn't someone else—than excited. My companion kneeled beside her and said her name too, but he spoke with little more than a whisper. Her eyes shot open and she looked at his face then mine, then both faces again. Horror overtook her. Her mouth opened but she didn't scream. She rolled to her right, knocking my companion off balance, and scrambled to her feet. She ran directly into the woods, disappearing into the thick green wall. Without even looking at me, my friend got to his feet and ran after her. I stood in the vacuum they left behind, in the place where this search began, and heard nothing, no sound at all.

A short time passed, and my friend reemerged from the foliage, his face scraped, the cuts filthy with dirt. Lucia was not with him.

"Are you . . . okay?" I didn't know how to respond to the last few minutes.

He wiped his face with an equally filthy hand and looked at me. Still pulling for air, he said, "You do know who she is?"

"Of course. My memory is not that unreliable."

His smirk suggested he didn't agree.

"Why was she here? In Baltimore. The one place she said she would never visit."

"You do know who she is?" he repeated.

"She so hated the very idea of coming here that she left . . . us. She left us simply because we came here. And now she's here?"

"She's here for you."

I looked away from him. The idea woke up something in me, as much as it scared me.

"She's here, Barney, because she is your sister."

"She found my sister?"

"She *is* your sister. And you know that."

I turned my back to him and looked into the park. It was open, clear and bright and open. So different from the trees behind me. I watched two children scurry behind their mother, whose pace was just a step too quick for them. I saw joggers in a loose line move along the packed dirt trail that crossed the park. A man pulled a large Igloo cooler and hawked "ice cold water."

I looked back at my friend. He was still huffing, but his eyes remained fixed on me. He hadn't asked a question, but he was waiting for some answer. I said the only thing I could say, the only thing I could possibly believe to be true: "No. She's not my sister."

BEFORE THE HITCHCOCK RESIDENCE
(LOS ANGELES, CA)

WHILE WE CAME TO BALTIMORE to find something, we occasionally heard of others who left the city for answers. A pair of local film-makers, favorites of graduate students and aesthetes but less than prolific in their own artistic production, encountered one another coincidentally (after several years of tacitly intentional estrangement) in front of the Bel Air mansion Alfred Hitchcock once called home, and in which he died. They had traveled from Baltimore to Los Angeles separately (one by plane and one by car) for different purposes (one for business and the other as a vacation). Both of them had taken the trip at substantial personal expense, and, despite the critical acclaim they both had garnered, neither was a rich man. Because of the struggle, each man had come to understand his own trip as a personal pilgrimage, and each had walked to Hitchcock's home with the hope of understanding how the man had lived. Upon meeting on that street, a regretful surprise for both of them, they shook firm hands, complimented each other's most recent films, and agreed that, once back in Baltimore, they would each watch the other's complete oeuvre then meet over crabs and canned beer to discuss their films at length. The problems began, however, when one of them suggested he would make a short film recreating this chance meeting before the Hitchcock residence, and the other stomped off in disgust, declaring that such an attempt to fix a moment was a mockery of the moment itself.

THE FARMER'S DAUGHTER

ONE SUNDAY AFTERNOON, in an effort to distract ourselves from our search for our missing siblings, we drove out to a large farmers' market far beyond the city's boundaries. One of the novelties this particular market boasted was freshly slaughtered meat, including, on that particular Sunday, rabbit, to be roasted or cooked into a stew. There is something about the nature of that animal, when living, that inspires emotional affection, especially in children. My companion and I bought two rabbits from the farmer who was selling them—he also offered a wide range of especially fresh produce, including mustard greens and Swiss chard—and he slit the rabbits' throats and prepared them for consumption with notable efficiency. As we left the market and walked to our car parked in the lot, we saw the farmer squatting beside his truck, hugging his young daughter, who was sobbing, obviously upset by the empty cages that were stacked beside her.

12

H E FOUND ME AT HOME. I was sitting in the dark, not exactly hiding. When he entered he flooded the kitchen with light. Unreflected overhead glare bore down on us. Without a word he kicked the chair from under me, forcing me to stand. He moved around so I could not look away. His face demanded an explanation, but I gave none.

He spoke of patience and respect that night. These were two things he had always offered me, and that I would not deny. He asked for the same. He said I had to respect that he had lost something too. Something that could still be found. And to do so, I would have to admit that I had found what I lost long ago. It was my responsibility to admit that I loved my sister in many different ways.

He must have known that what he asked me for in the kitchen that night was neither fair nor possible. If I said the words he asked me to say, then beyond any of the other complications (and those were many), he was asking me to give up my search, to say it was complete and had been for many years, and that in my state of denial, I had really only been helping him search for his brother. There was no sister to be found. She had left us already, before we ever made it to Baltimore.

I certainly could not speak. Anything I could have said at that moment would have been profane to his ears. All I could think to do was hold his hand, something I had never done before. I did just that and looked at his eyes. His fingers did not twitch or retract; they accepted my grasp. It was my hope this gesture could overcome the unspeakable. We looked each other in the eyes and shared our desperation and our sympathy.

"Your sister can find my brother," he said.

"I know."

He waited for me to speak. He wanted to hear me tell him that I knew she was my sister, and that I was ready to go find her.

Instead I said, "But we still haven't found my sister."

He dropped my hand and turned. I hadn't noticed that a small suitcase sat in the hall. He picked it up as he passed me, and then he walked out the door, letting it ease itself closed behind him.

Losing my friend frightened me. When I felt his desperation, those times when his face turned red, as it just had, I always felt the need to help him. If I had stated one simple idea aloud, I could have put his worries to rest. And I had been tempted to do just that, however horrifying the fact was. But I did not have the power to comfort him that day. I knew what help he needed, but I was also convinced that the truth, as he wanted it, was a lie.

DOMESTIC UNREST

A MANICURIST WHO—agitated by domestic unrest—lost control and strangled her husband to death (reportedly he was both a devout and angry man) was eventually freed from police custody. To the news cameras that waited for her as she exited the station, she held up her long-fingered hands and promised that as soon as she got home she would cut them both off and have them taxidermically preserved as a symbol of her proudest accomplishment. I told my companion that I could not even begin to conceive of ever experiencing such a total sense of closure.

GERTRUDE VESPUCCI'S STUDIO

A S AN EXTENDED SUMMER VACATION, a husband and wife who lived in Butcher's Hill but were rarely at home together (as she taught night classes at a community college during the week, and he traveled to sales conferences on the weekends), planned to travel to New Hampshire to visit an artisan's workshop and study the basics of the craft of stained glass for the whole month of August. They discussed their plan with their neighbors, a retired couple—friends of ours—who had visited the same workshop the summer before to learn rudimentary basket-weaving techniques, hoping the practice would have emotional, therapeutic consequences, and asked them for advice on how to best take advantage of their month in New England. Their neighbors suggested exactly what residence to stay in (one with a private toilet and shower) and insisted that they should study with Gertrude Vespucci, who was well known as the workshop's most loved instructor and who happened to teach stained-glass making. The neighbors went on to say that they themselves were considering a return to the workshop for the opportunity to sit in Ms. Vespucci's studio, even though their life had no room for another craft. The husband and wife drove north in August to learn a new skill and spend a full month together. Their neighbors had been right; the accommodations were basic but comforting, and sharing a bathroom with strangers was an unnecessarily excessive form of asceticism. But during their first week in Gertrude Vespucci's class, they both admitted that the pleasure their neighbors had promised was not to be found. She was an engaging and knowledgeable instructor—incredibly so, in fact. But her competence and the wonder she provoked served only as a reminder to the husband and wife that they experienced no feelings even remotely similar in each other's presence. They learned about the delicacy of cutting glass, the attention necessary to choose textures and colors, and the solidity of a piece after it has been well soldered, but each day in Gertrude Vespucci's studio served primarily to remind them that they would not be returning to Baltimore together.

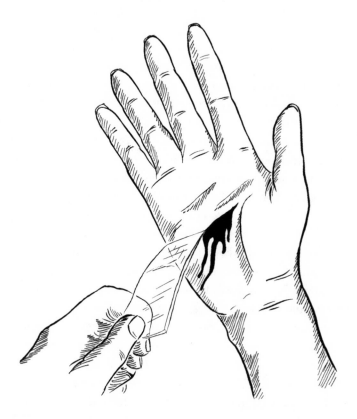

COMMUNITY SERVICE

THERE ARE CERTAIN THINGS we see often but never notice until they are broken, like the woman and her tenant who lived two doors down from the building we called home in Baltimore. This divorced woman, whose children had all left for college and beyond, acted unwisely in opening her home to a person in need of help. But, having seen how losing a child affected my own mother, I understood how a mother might desperately want to fill that void. This lonely woman offered, as a gesture of sympathy, her basement in-law suite to a "recovering drug addict," who was thrilled not to have to live in a shelter or under the stricture of a state-funded halfway house and was now, by this lonely woman's grace, given the opportunity to live in a stately row house, which even had a small yard where he could sit quietly and smoke cigarettes. The yard also had an outdoor grill on which he made a habit of preparing wonderful dinners for himself and his hostess almost every evening. She began to buy him clothes, vacuum his apartment, and treat him generally like her own son, who was studying marketing at Penn. We were all surprised on the day we stood witness to the recovering drug addict receiving two police cruisers outside of the woman's house and informing them that he had killed the woman who had, as a kindly gesture, offered him a place to sleep and eat. Poisoned, the coroner determined after the woman's body showed no obvious bodily trauma. When questioned by police as to why he would poison a woman who had been so kind to him, he said, "As a way of giving back to the community."

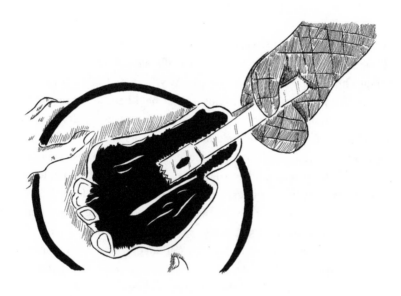

AT THE TAX PREPARATION OFFICE

THE MANAGER OF A TAX PREPARATION BUSINESS (a storefront operation) worried every day that he'd never make enough money to buy his family a home (they had rented for twenty years), and so, he revealed to my friend, his most trusted employee, that he'd been skimming profits during the confusion of the April tax season for several years, and that he had become quite fearful he'd be caught, and so he planned to leave the job before that happened and move his family to a less expensive city like Gainesville, Florida, or Phoenix, Arizona, where he could purchase a home with the modest sum he'd stashed away. He said that as soon as May 1 came and the office settled down again, he would tender his resignation, but he asked that my friend, who was, as he understood, a great sympathizer of his, not tell anyone about the money he had taken or his plan to leave. My friend, who for years had commiserated with his boss over Thursday-evening draft beers, said he'd keep his mouth shut, and in return, the boss promised him a promotion, a performance bonus, and even a modest share of the stolen money, once he and his family had safely reached Florida or Arizona. Before the lunch hour came that day, my friend had called the regional office to report his supervisor's theft. His boss was not only fired but also arrested, and my friend—as thanks for his corporate loyalty—was made manager of his office. By the end of May, he had fired and replaced any employee who had sympathy for his predecessor despite his crime, a majority of the staff. As for the accountant who reported the rumblings and grumblings of the staff to him in minute detail, he promoted him to assistant manager. Understanding the pattern of corporate ascendancy in the office, he planned to fire this man as soon as his restaffing was complete. But before that time came, his assistant placed his own call to the regional office to report my friend's cruel human resources practices, thereby ending his career in tax preparation.

CIVIC DUTY

ONE TUESDAY AFTERNOON, a well-known civic leader and charity worker dumped a whole bag of sandwiches on the side of the road, sandwiches intended for a community of homeless people who were set up beneath an old roadway overpass, because he could no longer bear to look at the misery of hopelessness directly. His assistants picked up the bag and ensured that everyone who was hungry was fed. The activist, though, was disingenuous about his faltering courage later that day, and offered many interviews with the local press discussing his role in *spearheading* an effort to *leave the soup kitchens and visit the streets,* and he even accepted an award for his work. On top of the civic award, the community activist, who was also a building contractor, accepted several contracts to install updated playgrounds in various city parks, contracts he surely secured because of his supposed charity. He even appeared on a local talk show with a former homeless man, boldly accepting the man's thanks and praise for his work with the city's destitute. It is impossible to know how many preeminent do-gooders lose their stomachs for working with the less fortunate each day and let their more modest compatriots finish the unsavory job, while still accepting fiscal favors and praise in the mass media, but you can assume it is about as many as community activists that exist. It is also necessary to note that there are just as many dedicated individuals who complete the service that has been offered by the more notable individual. As such, my companion and I have always preferred to accept the charity of quiet men and women who make few promises rather than the largesse of well-known civic leaders, and we have always been well fed. Sometimes we have even been satisfied.

13

SMALL INSTITUTIONS CONTROL LARGE MATTERS. So when I had to start my search again, this time alone, I began by attending a meeting of my local block association. I had seen a flyer taped to a parking sign with a date and address. I showed up at the house promptly on the stipulated day. It was a well cared for house with a small garden in front, the leaves green and the flowers all in bloom. I rang the bell and the host answered. She showed me to her dining room, where a group of concerned citizens sat around her fully extended table. They looked up at me, surprised by my appearance. Although the meetings were posted publicly, they didn't expect newcomers, especially childless itinerants like me. I suspect to most of them I was an unwanted interloper, but the ethical underpinnings of their social organization, as well as their own publicly argued standards, determined that they had to welcome me to their meeting, and, therefore, a few of them smiled when I sat down, while others nodded, and one even passed me a manila envelope holding five sheets of paper, including four flyers for various upcoming cultural events and one checklist that would function as an agenda for the night's meeting. As soon as I looked at the materials, someone handed me a package of Oreos, and someone else tipped a box of wine into a paper cup and offered me a drink. I thanked my fellow association members and sat back. I might have even dipped my cookie in the wine. I found it hard to understand how a group this irrelevant might be involved in the abduction of children.

I followed their discussions closely, even when references to specific zoning rules and regulatory boards threatened to lose me. I had enough experience in the courtrooms and other civic institutions of Baltimore to understand these civic machinations, at least vaguely. But I wasn't interested in street cleaning schedules or the optimal time to apply for a block party permit. Instead, I was studying the connections between the people sitting around me, looking for evidence of a secret shared.

The meeting itself revealed very little. I learned much more after I accepted an invitation to drink coffee with the select few who could afford not to run home to their families after the night's business had concluded. Our hostess, whose name, I learned, was Dorie, had baked a raspberry crumb cake that she put out with the coffee. It was delicious. If I knew how to bake, I would have asked for the recipe. Dorie and three other long-term neighborhood residents talked with each other and talked with me. They asked me how we were getting on in my friend's uncle's house. They asked about the garden, and if we had found the right stores to shop at and the right places to buy a cup of coffee or eat lunch. Conspicuously, none of them asked why we had to come to Baltimore, and, moreover, none of them asked about me. We can assume they understood my friend as a kind nephew doing a favor for his absent uncle, but surely they had to ask why an adult man like me would choose to suspend his life to house-sit in a strange city for a year or more. But they didn't. And that made me think they knew why I was there. Not only that, the fact that they avoided broaching the subject of my loss or my attempt to recover my sister led me to believe they already knew the details well, and, I suspected, knew many more details than I did. Surely the fact that I had shown up on their doorstep that night offered them a strategic advantage, as they could now keep tabs on me. It would be important, I decided, as I happily accepted the last piece of crumb cake, for me to hide my comings and goings from their vigilant watch. I finished the cake and stood. I thanked Dorie and her cadre of block association insiders and excused myself, leaving them behind to discuss me.

The sun had gone down, and when I crossed back to the house, I expected to find it dark. But in fact, two lights burned brightly. Rather than fear an intruder, I expected that my friend had returned. I hadn't seen him since he had left that afternoon weeks earlier. I rushed into the house, surprised by the elation I felt on the occasion of his return. I wanted to call his name, but I feared that might startle him. I wasn't sure he was ready to fully make amends. I walked into the front hallway and looked into the parlor, expecting he might be sitting on the couch reading old newspapers, as he had done most nights since we came to Baltimore. But the couch and the room were empty. I walked up the staircase to his bedroom, where I saw the other light on. The door was open, but still I knocked lightly, approaching him with caution. There was no response. I peeked inside and saw a pair of his shoes on the floor. I stepped in farther and saw his gray suit rumpled and discarded on a chair. I looked beside the bed, where he had collected stacks of manila folders, a makeshift filing cabinet for the evidence he had collected over the previous months and years, and saw that the folders were still there, but the stacks had been knocked over, and were now a mess of letter-sized paper and empty folders. Any semblance of a system he had been assembling was destroyed. I looked back at his shoes and saw that they were covered in mud. He usually kept his oxfords well polished and spotless. His suit looked as if he had run a marathon in it—not only was it wrinkled, but it was also covered with dark, wet stains, probably sweat, maybe some blood, maybe something else.

I stood in the middle of his room and listened for any noises in the house. Silence. My companion had returned, but at that moment, he was most certainly gone, most likely lost. I turned off the light in the room and shut the door, leaving my friend's decay behind me.

My suspicions about Dorie and her friends very quickly were proven true: they were concerned about my daily actions, and they had been watching me. In fact, Dorie did not take any remarkable measures to hide this fact. About a week after the first block meeting, I was sitting on my front stoop drinking a morning cup of coffee and taking notes about the patterns of the various municipal organizations that serviced our street on a given day (these are the kinds of institutions that could easily be exploited to conduct and cover up an extended series of abductions), when Dorie walked by, ostensibly tending to the small gardens in the tree pits that lined the block. She stopped and asked how my week had been. I told her I was fine, aware that it was important to reveal little to Dorie or any of her compatriots, who, I assumed, would rather I never find my sister.

Dorie sat on the step below me and told me she had been watching my yard. The previous weekend, she said, she had been having lunch with the Kaminskis, an older couple who lived two doors down from the house I was staying in and who had an impeccably maintained deck, the height of which surely broke one if not several zoning regulations. They had a clear view of the garden behind our house. She said that while they were eating lunch, they were alarmed to see a man down in that garden. The man, she said plainly, looked filthy, but, she observed, he did not look like someone who was used to being dirty, as, for instance, a homeless person or an auto mechanic might be. His clothes were freshly tattered, and the front of his shirt looked clean except for a few vivid stains. Despite observing these details, she assured me that she never saw the man's face. He sat in one of the lounge chairs and stayed there for several minutes, facing the vine-covered back wall, motionless. A squirrel came near him and he reached for it, as if to pet it, fully expecting it would stay put. When it darted away, as squirrels do, she noted, the man fell over, onto the lawn. Without brushing himself off, he crawled back onto the lounge chair, and this time he laid back. He closed his eyes and turned onto his side, as if he were sleeping on a bed. Then, she said, he stayed there for hours. My neighbor said that judging from his tossing and turning, he could not have been sleeping well. She and the Kaminskis finished their lunch and had coffee. They went inside and returned occasionally to check on this strange, sleeping man, but it wasn't until almost sundown that he finally left. They did not see him go.

"I thought to call you, to alert you," she said, "or, perhaps, to call over to the man. But I wasn't sure if he might be living there, in the house, with you."

"I see," I said.

"Is he, perhaps, the nephew?"

"Is he?"

"I thought you might know."

"But I never saw him," I informed her.

FRIENDLY REMINDER

A GENTLEMAN, whom we met at a party thrown by our friend at a downtown restaurant to celebrate her own birthday, sat at our table the whole evening (probably because he thought our occupations were funnier and our stories more interesting than those of the other partygoers, who were mostly our hostess's coworkers at the mortgage brokerage where she worked). At one point, he said he was feeling incredibly guilty, because just a week earlier, after noticing that his neighbor's curb was empty, he phoned the man, an aging widower, and offered him a friendly reminder to take out his trash, as the pickup would be early the next morning. His neighbor thanked him, and they both agreed it was astounding how trash could pile up if you missed even one pickup. As his neighbor finished dragging his bins from his rear garden to his curb, a car roared around the corner and collided with him at almost forty miles per hour, then crashed into the front of his house. Why the driver lost control is unclear, as the examination of her body showed no evidence of alcohol or drug consumption. From his kitchen in the rear of his house, our new friend had heard the crash and, he swore, the sound of the car's precise impact with his neighbor's body. The man admitted that the memory of the sound so haunted him that he had not slept for more than an hour at a time since the accident. He asked us whether we could remind him of what rest was like, but we felt it was not our place. We didn't mind distracting him with a humorous anecdote, but we weren't nearly familiar enough with him to fully resolve his troubled conscience (and my companion was slightly offended he would even ask).

SALESMAN

A T TIMES WE WOULD FEEL particularly alienated during our year in Baltimore. At those times, it took the example of those residents who remained there, despite having little to anchor them, to inspire us to persist. For instance, there was a Greek man who held the lease on a storefront on Eastern Avenue, and for some unknown reason did not have to be concerned about a regular income, according to a friend who worked at the city chamber of commerce. He had been operating a "treat stand," a store that purported to sell some kind of sweet, but indeed had not sold a single item in more than twenty years of operation, and, in fact, had never had a single item for purchase stocked on its shelves. The neighboring residents said that on most evenings, just after closing, the man closely inspected the empty shelves, apparently taking inventory, regularly noting things on a clipboard. My friend at the chamber of commerce said the man must have considered selling his business several years earlier, when he inquired at the local bank about having the value of his operation determined. Afraid of embarrassing him, the bank employee politely suggested that it would be more lucrative to operate the store himself, and he accepted this advice. At the height of the midsummer heat, for two weeks each year, he closed down the store and, according to a cardboard sign that hung in its window, traveled to Maryland's Eastern Shore. It was an escape from the doldrums, quiet, and oppressive humidity of August in Baltimore.

SEASON TICKETS

THE ORIOLES SEASON TICKETS that we bought during our time in Baltimore afforded us an ideal view of the field, but everything else about our seats was unfortunate, particularly the pair of season ticket holders who sat to our left, who were obnoxious in every meaning of the word. They even made it difficult to enjoy watching the shortstop's MVP season play out before us. After learning that their son had been abducted seven years earlier, and that they still stayed awake past midnight every night, hoping for his return, we still loathed them and asked to have our seats moved.

A NEW FRIEND IN ATLANTIC CITY

WHILE IN BALTIMORE, I found it helpful to keep my appearance neat and orderly as a means of staying focused on my search, and, as such, I visited a barber once every two weeks. My barber told me about his nephew, who had recently driven to Atlantic City and said that as he drove into town—while looking in the darkened windows of the pawnshops and motels on the city's ground level—he decided that rather than stay at an affordable hotel and gamble with the modest amount of money he had put aside for that purpose, he would stay in the most opulent room his credit card could gain access to at the Borgata, then rely on his luck at the craps tables to pay the eventual bill. He truly admired the polarity of Atlantic City and found a sharp, almost painful excitement in the city's constant tension, an excitement unequaled by even the decadence of Las Vegas, which he had visited once for a long weekend, but found its endless pleasure and *adult-imitation child wonder* (as he referred to it) so boring that he vowed never to set foot in the state of Nevada for the rest of his life. Less than half an hour after entering Atlantic City, my barber's nephew found himself at a craps table. As the night went on, he roamed from table to table, casino to casino, sometimes making money, but more often making new friends. He had rolled dice at so many different tables that he couldn't imagine there was one in the whole city that he hadn't visited. By sunrise, he had done well, but he still had neither reached his goal of covering the cost of his suite at the hotel, nor had he lost enough money to have it paid for. Eventually, though, he told my barber that he met a man with a corporate card who told him not to worry about the room, he would have it comped—and the man did just that with a quick call to the concierge. He then invited my barber's nephew and several young women back to his own suite at the Borgata for mimosas and scrambled eggs. They all followed him to the suite and settled into the abundance of couches in his sitting room. He passed around mimosas and proposed a toast to Fortune. The young women drank, but the barber's nephew did not, as he didn't like champagne. Quickly the laughter and chatter in the room fell to silence. The young man looked at the women—each of them sat stiff and empty-eyed. It did not take him long to realize that they were all dead. He looked for his host, who was gone, and as he surveyed the sitting room, he realized that no less than a half dozen more well-dressed young men and women sat stiff and dead along the walls of the room. Their faces betrayed neither the horror nor the pleasure of their final moments, just a notable absence of life. He must have missed them in the morning's dusky light. He immediately ran to the hotel's front desk to inform them of the tragic situation in their presidential suite. Security checked the suite immediately and found nothing but the man with the corporate card quietly eating his breakfast. My barber's nephew headed straight to his car and drove directly out of Atlantic City. He has yet to return to the town that he once loved.

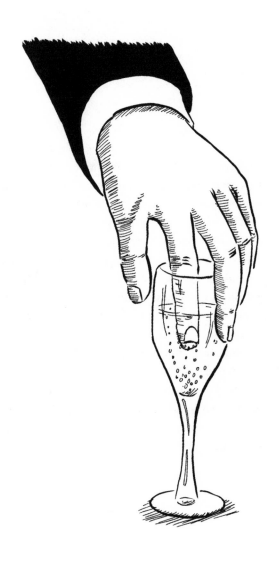

FAILURE TO SAVE

B ECAUSE HE HAD BEFRIENDED A LOCAL PASTOR who sat with him on the school board (the pastor was a community leader who was equally respected by those in the homeless shelters and those in city hall), a man who was a tax accountant from Roland Park began to preach before the pastor's congregation on occasional Sundays, offering sermons that, according to the congregants, were inspired but almost completely incomprehensible, and, therefore, uninspiring. The tax accountant stopped attending his friend's church on Sundays, as he was so disheartened by his failure to move and *save* the people sitting in the pews. Several months after the tax accountant's final Sunday in the pulpit, the pastor's weekly sermon was interrupted by smoke coming from the church parking lot. In response, the entire congregation ran outside to find the tax accountant standing there, blank-faced, before a stack of paperback Bibles that he had set on fire, a fire that was quickly spreading among the surrounding trees, and which the tax accountant then resignedly walked into. The churchgoers screamed, unable to prevent him from fully immolating himself.

FIRST DAUGHTER

THE DAUGHTER OF A FORMER CONGRESSMAN, with whom I had had a drink at the local lounge on several occasions, explained that her father had left office midterm, a shock to all his constituents—as he was a shoe-in for reelection—because on his wedding day he had made a promise that he would retire to Georgia with his wife on the day that their firstborn, who was the daughter I knew, turned thirty-five and became eligible for the presidency of the United States. Those who knew of the promise, including his wife, never imagined he would make good on it, as his wife was very happy with their life in Maryland, and their daughter had no aspirations to the presidency or any sort of public office. So, they were all surprised when he did, in fact, step down from office on his daughter's thirty-fifth birthday, and soon relocated to a gated golf community on Jekyll Island in Georgia. Despite the unnecessary nature of his move, he stuck to his plan and never even left the state of Georgia. His experience was probably maddening, depressing, or at least boring in some way, evidenced by the fact that on his daughter's fortieth birthday, while she was visiting her parents to celebrate, he went out for a swim and drowned himself in the very calm ocean. I asked his daughter if she could explain his choice, and she said that the night before his death, she asked him if he ever regretted his move to Georgia, and he said he had never questioned it for a moment. He said anyone who examined such a choice in any way was liable to be driven mad with regret and the looming presence of possibility.

MOTHER'S INTUITION

MY COMPANION AND I used to end up in the first hours of many Sunday mornings at a club called the Flamingo on East Baltimore Street. One such morning, we shared a bottle of bourbon with a particular exotic dancer, who told us about the near horrors of her school years, horrors that made us wonder if our long-lost brother and sister were better off for having gone missing while still so young. On the day of the Rumson Street Children's Massacre, as the newspapers called it, fifteen members of the dancer's third-grade class were killed and six others fell ill, all because of poisoned cupcakes an angry father sent his daughter to school with on her ninth birthday. Then, in high school, four members of the volleyball team, of which she was the captain, were raped by a bitter young math teacher, who imprisoned them in the girls' locker room and held them at gunpoint (the gun, it was later learned, was a fake). I asked her how she had avoided these notorious tragedies, and she gave all the credit to her mother (for whom she had no other kind words), who often claimed to receive premonitions from her television set. They were almost always inaccurate, but on both of these occasions, the messages told her to insist that her daughter stay home from school the next day. Ultimately, the dancer admitted, although she had not fallen victim to these crimes, the debt her mother expected from her for her lucky intuitions was so unreasonable, and had created so much anger, that she often wished she had not been spared on either of those horrible days.

14

WORKING WITH THE BLOCK ASSOCIATION certainly enhanced my civic engagement, which meant attending rallies, which are the precursors to political fundraisers. At political fundraisers for local figures, the candidates are expected to engage the attendees in actual conversation, though cursory and polite. It was at one such fundraiser, which I was asked to attend because I chaired the local green space cleanup committee, that I met Ronald, our city council representative. Ronald had mayoral aspirations, and from what the veterans of Baltimore's political game told me, his hopes were not completely foolish. He was a friendly and likable figure whose particular vulnerability was excess candor. This was clearly the man I needed to befriend if I hoped to gain any insights into the specific political machinations involved in the abductions. Not only did he wield considerably more influence than my immediate neighbors, but his frequent lapses in discretion were, in effect, a series of opportunities for me to peek behind the curtain as well. So when, at the fundraiser, he invited me to a dinner to learn about a "community action group" he was assembling, I gladly accepted. After that dinner, when the half-finished personal pizzas and plates of penne had been cleared, and Ronald had retired to the bar for one more drink, I found a stool next to him. He was drinking Cutty Sark on the rocks, and I bought him another, which he gladly accepted. We talked until the restaurant closed, and I never mentioned my sister even once. Neither did he.

After that, he began to invite me for dinner or drinks on most nights, and, whenever possible, even on nights that I had committee meetings, I accepted. Like most men of his age and position, he didn't like being alone, and, moreover, he was especially afraid of being alone with his family. I was only too glad to take advantage of this susceptibility, and, night after night, over countless lamb chops and scotches, he began to trust me.

Not long after our partnership began, he invited me to partake in his favorite pastime: spending long, dark nights in Baltimore's strip clubs. By exposing himself in this way to me, it ensured not only that he trusted me, but also that he was indebted to me for my discretion. One particular night, after a long dinner, we walked to one of these clubs, the one where, he said, he felt most comfortable, because most of the dancers knew him, and, therefore, knew when to approach him and when to let him drink quietly. A few women did come by the table that night, but they only said hello, sat, and watched the stage beside us, then moved on.

My stomach felt warm from the drinks with dinner, and the drinks after dinner, and the councilman appeared particularly content. I hadn't planned it, but I chose that moment to reveal that I had lost my sister. He kept his eyes on the dancer onstage—who hung upside down from a pole—and nodded as if he already knew. I suspected he did already know, and hoped so, if he, in fact, had the influence and insight I thought he did. I told him I was sure there were people who knew exactly what had happened to my sister and so many others, and I asked if he could help me.

"There are people who know," he said, clapping for the dancer. "In many ways I know, or could know exactly. I've learned to remain ignorant more often than not. Knowing too much is often more dangerous than not knowing enough."

"Could you help me?"

"I can find your sister. Or, at least, find out about her."

I leaned back, elated. It was the first progress I had made since seeing Lucia in the woods.

"But I'm not going to," he said. "That wouldn't help you." He pulled his eyes from the stage and put a hand on my shoulder. "You don't want to deal with everything that comes along with finding your sister."

"How would you know?"

"You think you're the first person I've known who's gone down this path? I'm a nice guy, Barney. I've helped people with this in the past. Against my better judgment. I've walked with them right down to that warehouse by the river. Who knows what's even inside it? It doesn't go well. It never goes well."

This was the first I'd heard of a warehouse. I finished my drink in one swallow.

Ronald looked at me, and I could see that it was hard for him to watch my struggle. After all, this was a man whose stock-in-trade was satisfying people. There was nothing that would have made him happier than telling me he would take care of the matter. Finally, he relented. He pulled the napkin from under his drink and pushed it toward me. He took a pen out of his jacket and handed it to me. "Write down her name," he said. "Right here. I'll see what I can do."

I didn't hesitate and wrote her name neatly on the damp napkin.

He folded it up and put it in his jacket. As he did, he yawned. "Is it about that time?" he said.

On our way out, he asked if I would step into the dressing rooms with him. "There's a girl I need to speak to," he said. Ronald was kind to the people he cared about. He often helped dancers at the clubs with small legal complications or personal matters.

We went into the dressing room, which was full of mostly clothed women. The reversal of habit that occurred at a strip club struck me as funny: the dancers take off their clothes outside and cover up in private. Some of the women were busily applying make-up and talking with each other about how busy things had been. In the back of the room, one woman was crying loudly. There was a disheveled man in a suit comforting her, his hand on her back, but, judging from her shudders and sobs, he wasn't succeeding.

The councilman noticed immediately and asked, "What's the problem here?"

The disheveled man looked up at us—it was my absent companion, Thomas. His face registered no surprise at seeing me. He simply frowned, at a loss to help the sad woman.

The councilman didn't hesitate to get involved. He kneeled down before her in his tight-fitting suit and held her hand. "What's the problem, Grace?" he said.

"My brother," she muttered, "and his brother." She nodded at my tired-looking friend. "I almost found him. And then I didn't. And I tried to forget."

"As you should," the councilman said, stroking her back.

"But then, this man"—she nodded at my friend—"started talking about his brother, and how he lost him, and I remembered the night at the warehouse."

The councilman shot a glance at my friend, then back at me. He shook his head, aware that he was piloting a ship of fools who wouldn't leave well enough alone. He looked back at the woman, who had begun to compose herself. "I should have never taken you there. We didn't know what was inside. We *don't* know what was inside."

"I know," she said. "I've done everything to forget that it's there, that my brother is gone, or ever was here. But I meet this guy and he starts talking about his brother and asking about the warehouse and . . ." Her sobs seized her again.

The councilman looked at my friend. "Who are you?"

"A guy who's very close to finding something he lost."

The councilman looked at me. "Isn't everybody?"

My friend kneeled before the woman and held her hands. "Please," he said. "Tell me where this place is, this warehouse, and I promise you'll never hear another word from me. Whatever I do or don't find, you won't hear from me."

"Don't," the councilman ordered. "That's a hornets' nest we should never have kicked."

I stepped in. "Then you tell us, Ronald."

He looked back at me, confused by my assertiveness. "Are you kidding me here?"

"I'm not. Tell us where it is and there's no need for us to talk about anything to anyone."

The politician looked around the strippers' dressing room and sighed. "I'll tell you where it is. I don't know how you think it'll help you, knowing where this warehouse is. But let's agree right now: I never want to hear another word about this. Like he said, whatever you do—or, more likely, don't—find, I don't want to hear about it."

I happily agreed. This was all I needed. He then described, in great detail, a wooded spot off of the highway.

My companion and I walked out onto the fluorescent-lit street together that night. We didn't go home. We followed the directions we had just been given.

FIRST IN LINE AT THE PEEPSHOW

DOWN ON BALTIMORE STREET, after spending several daylight hours at a bar, two college friends, who had attended the University of Maryland in their younger years, entered an adult entertainment arcade and stood before a live peepshow booth. Despite being slightly embarrassed, they both agreed that the women available were remarkably beautiful, and they assured each other that sensuality this rare was worth paying for. They both chose the same small dark-haired woman to watch, and, so as not to seem overly eager or perverse, they also both insisted that the other go first. At last they agreed that the married man, who, as such, was the more desperate of the two, should enter the private booth first. He was astounded by what the woman showed him when they were behind the curtain. He stumbled from the booth delirious with pleasure. But his bachelor friend began to sob once he himself was behind the curtain, a sob that slowly became a violent choking sound. The married man threw open the curtain to find his friend's lifeless body before him, while the naked woman still performed, her eyes closed, unaware of what had happened on the other side of the glass. The man who survived, and whom we met one late night at a bar, said he still often thinks about this moment and wonders what his friend saw in the woman's dance that he himself did not.

BESIDE THE NEW JERSEY TURNPIKE

B ALTIMORE'S GREATEST PUBLIC SERVANT, a former city councilman, was found dead in the woods of southern New Jersey, having fallen down a steep hill. He was killed either by the traumatic impact of his descent or from blood loss as he lay on the dead autumn leaves after he fell. We had hosted this man in our home on several evenings; we were inspired by his understanding of city politics and by his explanations of how the state of political affairs had become so abject, a reality that chilled everyone at the table. Oddly enough, it was in his truthful but grim descriptions that we began to develop a hope that this man could be the one person in Baltimore to help us find our lost siblings. But, because he was a publicly thoughtful and complicated man, he was voted out of office after a single term, and had failed in several subsequent bids for a local position. When we learned he had died, we began to see the shadows growing across our chances of leaving Baltimore with any sort of resolution, but we also recalled that he had been our first true friend in the city. He was a tireless critic of the local social structure and never hesitated to inform the *Sun* of his specific opinions concerning his lesser colleagues. We sympathized with him because, like us, he had always accepted misery with open arms and understood that he could only serve by dedicating himself to sharing this misery. The cause of his fall was unclear, and many assumed his death was a suicide because of the pain in which he had lived his life. These people, who insist that he killed himself, also insist that his tragedy was a result of his *attitude* in life, while a fair analysis would, in reality, reveal that he was ruined by the ignorance of his city, which shut him up as it has so many.

UTILITY

FOLLOWING A HUNCH that my companion had during the early, grasping days of our search, we took a weekend-long trip to a town in the mountains where, even today, sewage and sanitation is not fully advanced, and, because of their fragile plumbing systems, many residents often choose to relieve themselves outdoors, especially when urinating. In the small downtown area, this practice caused an obvious odor and cleanliness problem, and, as such, certain merchants, particularly men, exercise the practice of urinating into jars, which they then empty near their homes outside of town. Up there, there's open space and substantial distance from their neighbors. Those who live lower in the mountains than others complain that the urine runs down onto their property, but other more enterprising residents have taken advantage of the situation to grow vegetable gardens, understanding that the urine wards off would-be predators, animals that would otherwise make growing a garden almost impossible. My companion swore that the urine wasn't the only odd smell in town; it also smelled of a child's fear. We thought we saw a photograph of his missing brother on the mantle in the living room of the bed-and-breakfast where we stayed. But our hostess assured us that the boy in the picture was not my companion's lost brother, but her own nephew, who lived in Santa Fe. We accepted her story politely, but my companion's eyes revealed a clear doubt that this woman could possibly have a nephew living in New Mexico.

HAMMOND'S VIEW

THE COLUMNIST ED HAMMOND, whom my companion and I came to know well during our time in Baltimore (until he resigned from the paper and moved to North Africa), and whose talents included not just unapologetic political criticism but also an ability to coerce prominent politicians into embarrassing admissions with well-timed anonymous phone calls to their private lines, swore to me during our long and mostly silent walks through Fell's Point in the dead of many midwinter weeknights that bodies of no fewer than seven former mayoral hopefuls were buried beneath the cobblestones of the exact streets on which we walked, and that the murder of political opponents was a strongly adhered-to Baltimore tradition carried on for generations. I asked several of my friends, all longtime city residents, if they were familiar with this tradition. Each rolled his or her eyes, unwilling to discuss the matter. But Hammond's written legacy will prove that he never once found it necessary to stretch the truth in an effort to characterize the horror of the ambition he observed.

BAND SHELL

IN PATTERSON PARK, a band shell was built as a place to hold free concerts, an undertaking the city felt assured would be quite profitable. One man climbed a tree for an ideal vantage point of the concert grounds, which were vacant at the time, and swore that he heard an orchestra playing Wagner's *Faust Overture*. He returned to the tree regularly, and every time he clearly heard the orchestra, a fact that he was shy to disclose, as he questioned his own sanity. Eventually, he shared his experience with a few close friends, after he had heard several dozen performances and could no longer doubt himself. Because these friends, and then their friends, and eventually even the guided tours of the city began to visit the trees surrounding the band shell, and everyone heard the invisible music just as the man had, people stopped attending the scheduled concerts inside the fence, and the city began to lose considerable money on the venture. In a plot supposedly hatched by members of the city government and several labor unions, the man who had first heard the music was abducted and either relocated or killed, although the evening news simply reported him as missing. We well understood that despite certain inefficiencies in the Baltimore city government, it was particularly adept at obscuring the details of disappearances, abductions, kidnappings, and the like. The original chain-link fences, which were meant to create a subtle outline of the concert space that wouldn't disrupt the venue's natural and verdant setting, were replaced with cement barriers, and the surrounding trees were cut down, their stumps completely ground down so as to remove any suggestion of their existence. After several poorly attended seasons, the performances in the band shell were canceled and the cement structure was allowed to fall into disrepair.

15

WE PULLED OUR CAR to the side of highway exactly where the councilman had told us to. I looked into the woods and saw nothing but darkness. I was convinced we had been tricked, or at least the information we had been given was inaccurate, but before I could say so, my companion ran into the woods. I had no choice but to follow.

Not a few hundred feet into the trees there was, indeed, a very large building, probably a warehouse. No lights came from within it, and, certainly, no lights illuminated it from outside. It was a long-abandoned building, a cement box in the woods, from what I could tell, that expected no visitors. Any road that led to it from the highway had been long ago claimed by the forest floor, and any footpaths, planned or improvised, were grown over. I followed my friend's footsteps until we got to the structure's outer wall. I thought we would never be able to find an entrance, let alone unlock one, but he set to testing every seam he could find, and eventually he found a door, one that opened fairly willingly with a firm push. He held it open for me and we both went inside.

A bright light, cold and blue, greeted us. By the time our eyes adjusted, we realized we were in some sort of bare receiving room. There was a cement floor and a bank of elevators across from us. From far off, we heard the buzz of an excited crowd. None of these signs of life had been apparent from the building's exterior. Still, the room we stood in was empty: no furniture, no fixtures, no people, just fluorescent lights, cement, and a far-off din. My companion approached the elevators and searched for a call button, while I stood just inside the entrance, trying to evaluate whether I was in the midst of some delusion. He found no button and began to search the walls to see if there was some inconspicuous doorway that led to a staircase. He found nothing. A few moments later, we heard the soft "ding" of the elevator and one of the doors eased open. Inside was a young girl of no more than eleven or twelve years old. We both froze, shifting only our eyes between the girl and one another. She stepped out of the elevator and crossed the lobby, offering us a cursory glance and the slightest nod. As she approached the door we had just entered, my companion found his voice.

"Excuse me, miss."

She stopped and looked at us, smiling politely.

"Could you tell us"—he wasn't sure what he wanted to know—"how to get upstairs?"

She looked directly at me and said, "Are you looking for your sister?"

My words died before I could speak them.

"Yes," my friend helped me. "Yes, he is."

"Take the elevator to the third floor." She smiled again and stepped out into the wooded darkness beyond the door.

My friend hopped into the elevator before the doors could close. I followed him slowly, unsure if I should believe what I was just told. He pressed the only lit button in the bank, the one that read "3," and a moment later the doors quietly closed. I looked to my friend as the elevator rose, expecting his reassurance or interpretation, any response to our experience, but he simply watched the numbers above the doors, probably anxious that the doors wouldn't actually open when we reached the third floor. But they did.

We stepped out into a long corridor, painted a pale gray and lit overhead with more unapologetically industrial lighting. It felt like a self-storage facility, except for the cheerful sound of children's voices, which could be heard distinctly coming from somewhere on the floor. My companion began to walk down the corridor and I followed quickly, afraid the elevator doors might shut and I might lose whatever opportunity had been presented to me.

He saw something up ahead and began to jog, then he stopped and turned toward a wall. When I caught up, I realized that he wasn't facing a wall, but a window, a large observation window that looked into a room, a room full of children sitting at long tables. Most of the children, who ranged from toddlers to teenagers, sat on benches and seemed to be enjoying a meal. I checked my watch; it was four thirty in the morning. A few of them shuttled trays of food and plates between the tables and a set of swinging doors at the rear of the room. Despite the hour, this cafeteria was in full swing.

"Can they see us?" my friend asked.

I tapped the glass lightly, but there was no response. I banged it again with my knuckles. Still nothing. I pounded the thick glass with my fist, and not a single child turned his head. But, a moment later, we heard a distinct sound rise above the others. One of the children was shouting something, the same word again and again. I looked to see who it was and couldn't tell. None of the children seemed to acknowledge the sound. It got louder, and I strained to hear what the child was calling for. It was the same two syllables, over and over. As it got louder, I thought the sound, the word, the intonation, was familiar.

My friend looked at me. "Your name," he said. "She's calling your name."

I wasn't sure, but soon it became clear: some girl inside was calling, "Baaar-neeey, Baaar-neeey, Baaar-neeey."

I needed to find a way to this voice, but the window was sealed. My friend pointed farther down the corridor. A door was opening and a boy walked out, a very young child, no more than six years old. We watched as he approached; he didn't seem to notice us until he passed. When he did, he mumbled something that sounded like "hello" and continued to the elevators. He disappeared into the one that was waiting. The sound of my name grew louder.

As soon as the boy was gone I ran to where he had emerged. I pushed on the door and it swung in, allowing me into the cafeteria. Inside, the din of dozens of children eating dinner was far greater. But, in turn, the sound of my name ringing above the white noise was far clearer. There was no question that the word the girl kept repeating was *Barney*.

I began to go up one aisle, and the voice got louder. But then it began to fade. I moved down another, and another, but I could get no closer. I looked back to see if my companion had followed me into the cafeteria.

He was stepping into the room when he fell back violently. It was as if he tripped backwards. Then I saw arms grab him, the full-grown arms of an adult man, or men. He was pulled from the room. With my name ringing in my head, I ran to the door, to my friend's aid. Back in the corridor, I saw two men dressed completely in dark colors, dragging him away.

"Stop!" I shouted, but before I could take another step, I found myself knocked to the ground, the dark sleeve covering a man's forearm across my eyes. I was dragged behind my friend through a doorway that led to a staircase. The men who dragged us were efficient; they said not a word, not even a grunt or yelp. They braced us both so tightly that we couldn't offer even the most basic of struggles. As they carried us down the stairs, my heels bumping against each step, I heard my name, repeated as persistently as ever. Then it faded away. Finally, we were ushered through the lobby downstairs and thrown out the way we came in.

Outside, the sun had begun to rise, and frosty steam came off the fallen leaves. In the early light, we could see the building we had just been inside of, and it was clearly a warehouse. But as before, we could detect no sound, no light, no life from within. My name was trapped behind the heavy door we'd just been shoved through.

I ran back to the door and pushed on it, but there was no give. It was now locked. My friend grabbed my shoulder before I attempted to open it again.

"The night's over," he said.

I looked at the sun appearing through the trees, and I looked at his tired face and dirty clothes. "It is," I agreed, and started to follow our trail back to our car.

FAILURE AND SUCCESS

ON HIS RETURN FROM A BUSINESS TRIP TO OHIO, where he'd been try-ing to sell HVAC systems to large businesses, my neighbor, a man of complicated but well-considered artistic taste, had bought a novel to read during the plane flight home, which he had then lent to me and which I, in turn, had shared with my companion. Once we had all read the novel, we sat down to eat grilled hamburgers in our small yard and the topic of the book naturally came up. I described the narrative as a complete suc-cess, while my companion called it an unmitigated failure. My companion described the plot's total lack of resolution as completely unbearable, while I cited that exact fact, the book's admission of our ultimately dissatisfied psyches, as a welcome—and, in fact, necessary—overture. Our neighbor, mopping up the ketchup on his plate with a bit of hamburger bun, said that both of us made very convincing arguments.

CRIMINAL NEGLIGENCE

THE OCTOBER BEFORE WE ARRIVED in Baltimore, almost one hundred recent ex-convicts were killed, not due to a revenge plot or crime-related incident, but because of a wilderness survival trip that was organized as a means of learning the discipline and skills necessary for reintegration into the community. The trip leader, a former prison guard, compelled the men (despite their protests) to cross a rotted wooden bridge that spanned a gap three hundred feet above a stream that had run shallow due to a recent drought. The bridge gave way after only a handful of men (including the trip leader) had successfully crossed it. The families of the deceased accused the man of criminal negligence, and to this day still hope that he himself will be a convict before another year has passed. As time went on, my companion and I became increasingly convinced that these mourners, like most people, will not be able to get the satisfaction they expect.

LEGS

THE MORE TIME WE SPENT in Baltimore, the more we came to understand the city's unique ability to take children from their parents in increasingly indirect and unforeseen ways, as in the case of a high school English teacher, whose choice to conduct a relationship with his seventeen-year-old student must have been a result of poor judgment provoked by his anxiety about turning forty. The girl was an only child of a single mother, and an aspiring track star with the promise of a full scholarship to any number of universities. Her mother always saw her daughter's legs as her most valuable asset, and she understood that she might never be able to use them again, so, when she was moved to exact revenge on the English teacher who had taken advantage of her daughter, she decided that a set of legs was the exact reparation she deserved. She hired a man who visited the teacher in the faculty lounge and explained that he was going to cut off his legs, and he did, calmly and surgically. After the details of the affair came out, the English teacher had not only his legs taken from him, but his job as well. At the time that he was attacked, he didn't understand why anyone would wish such a cruel punishment on him, until he learned a week later, as he emerged, legless, from the trauma of the event, that his seventeen-year-old student and lover had swallowed several bottles of pills after her mother had learned of their affair and pledged to get both school and legal authorities involved. The girl put herself into a coma from which she never woke.

FIVE CLOWNS

A GROUP OF FIVE UNDERPAID CLOWNS came up with the idea of designing an act that they could book and perform at small clubs and bars around the city, as the rote buffoonery they were required to execute night after night at the circus under the big top had become dull and painful to them. They all met one night in a local café, without makeup and floppy shoes, with the intention of planning the delicate orchestration of their routine, but arranging a performance that features five different performers is a difficult thing to coordinate. Each brought a very specific—and very different—concept that would draw the crowd's amusement and amazement to himself or herself. After months of meetings at the café, the five clowns had cobbled together their disparate ideas into a single show for which they could conceive of no better title than *Clowning Around,* and, almost a year after the day they had come up with the idea, they began performing their show regularly on Thursday nights at a trendy lounge downtown. My companion and I had the misfortune of seeing one of these shows. After their first month of performing, the crowds dwindled to almost nothing, as the show was just sloppy and unorganized enough to embarrass the audience rather than amuse it. Incompetence, if particularly exaggerated, can certainly aid a clown's performance. In the case of these five clowns, their failure was pedestrian and unremarkable. As such, their residency at the lounge was abruptly ended.

16

B Y THE TIME WE WOKE after the night in the warehouse, it was midday. I met my friend in the kitchen. We were home together for
the first time in weeks. I offered him coffee. We both sat at the
same table and looked out the windows with a shared sense of
anxiety and focus. At that moment I could have asked him where he had
been for so many weeks, what trouble he had gotten into, if he had found
Lucia, if he still insisted on the corrupted nature of our relationship, if he
was any closer to finding his brother. But at that moment, I was wholly
occupied by what I had seen in that warehouse, and, more specifically,
what I had heard. I wanted to suggest that we return, but I feared my friend
would think that imprudent or purposeless. We drank our coffee in silence
until he stood and said, "Let's go back."

My friend's eyes were clearer at that moment than they had been since
we came to Baltimore. He drove while I watched our path through the
city, which looked transformed in the daylight. In the night the path had
been simple, like a tunnel, but in the day, the colors were vivid and the
physical elements distinct, all competing for my attention. We pulled onto
the highway and things began to simplify. Broken cityscape gave way to
blacktop and foliage, regular and natural. And then we came to that spot
on the shoulder where we had parked the night before. The trees were
clearer and more picturesque in the daylight, but the warehouse was no
easier to see, as its pale vastness spread behind the leaves, a backdrop as

unobtrusive and ubiquitous as the sky itself. I must have driven past the place at least a dozen times and never noticed the massive building just off the road.

Without so much as looking at me, my companion opened the car door and headed into the trees. I hurried after him. We fully expected a struggle when we tried to reenter the building. The men who'd ejected us the night before had acted with such confidence and ability that we understood they would allow us to enter, but to see nothing they didn't wish us to.

I approached the door we'd entered through the first time and touched it tentatively. I pulled down on the handle, waiting to feel the resistance of its lock, but instead I felt the click of an opening latch. I pushed slightly and the door opened, as easily as it had the night before.

Once inside, we were greeted by the same receiving room, clean and bright and lonely and cold. We could hear the children's voices coming from above. One elevator in the bank remained open, and we stepped inside before we missed our opportunity. Once again, the only lit button on the panel was "3," and my companion pushed it. As the elevator rose we heard the din of the cafeteria grow louder. The mood seemed even more energetic and raucous than the night before. I wondered when these children slept. My companion watched the numbers light up as we hit the second floor, and I knew he didn't trust that we would arrive on the third floor again, that we'd be able to access what we had already found. But, as it had the night before, the elevator stopped on the third floor and the doors opened.

Stepping off, I strained to hear my name again, shouted above all the other shouts and screeches and laughs. Instead, as if in response to our arrival, the children's voices almost immediately quieted to complete silence. We rushed to the window to see what might have prompted this lull, but when we got there, we found an empty room. The tables still sat there in clinically neat rows, but the children were gone, the food was gone, and the voices were all gone. My companion and I both turned instinctively, prepared for the men to grab us again, but there was no one there, just a long, brightly lit hallway. I looked through the window again, to see if some trace of the night before remained, but there was none. I pressed my ear to the glass, hoping to hear at least a fading voice, one of a young girl calling my name, but that too was an empty desire.

My friend headed back to the elevator. I ran to follow him and had to stick my foot out to prevent the door from closing. I entered and stood beside him. "Where do we look now?" I asked.

He didn't reply, just watched the numbers count down until we returned to the ground floor. He walked out of the elevator toward the building's front door. When he reached it, he paused and said, without turning, "There's nowhere left to look. We got too close, and we weren't prepared, and now we've missed our chance." And with that, he left.

Again I pursued him. Once outside, I saw my friend walking farther into the woods, away from the road. I knew nothing could be gained by following him and understood that he wouldn't be coming back. I looked at the warehouse and saw that whatever doors might open inside it, it was as impenetrable as its outer walls made it seem. Alone once again, I walked back to the road, no closer to the person I had lost, with little reason left to continue my days in Baltimore.

LAB PARTNERS

UNRESOLVED ENDINGS and unanswered desperation in Baltimore are not features unique to the cases of my companion and me. A physics graduate student, Ms. Tankleff, witnessed the death of her fellow graduate student, Ms. Tartikoff, on a daylong hiking trip to western Maryland. She reported that it was *an accident* that occurred when they left the marked trail and Ms. Tartikoff fell into a ditch that was hidden by the pitch of the verdant ground they were crossing. Ms. Tankleff reached for her friend as she began to slip, but had to let go when she realized that she too would be pulled into the ditch, which was more than fifty feet deep with a slate bottom. Ms. Tartikoff died immediately when her head crashed into the ditch's floor, fracturing her neck and skull. Ms. Tankleff explained that she and Ms. Tartikoff had worked in the same lab and went on regular hiking trips together. When interviewed about the case by police, though, their professors and fellow students claimed the two women hadn't gone hiking together in months and, in fact, never spoke inside the lab except when absolutely necessary, and hadn't since Ms. Tartikoff was awarded a lucrative research assistantship for which Ms. Tankleff had also applied and not received. Three people had died in the same state park in the previous two years, and it was understood that crimes committed even in patrolled wilderness were more difficult to detect than those committed in the city due to the lack of electronic surveillance and nature's efficiency in destroying evidence.

TIME-SHARE

AFTER YEARS OF DEBATING HOW to spend their excess savings—whether to buy a bungalow on the shore or a cabin in the mountains, a debate that ruined the lives of both their children and their extended family—a certain couple, husband and wife, finally invited the wife's cousin to invest in their vacation property with them. Eventually, they admitted to him that they had been torn for so long on the issue that they knew they would never decide. This caused such a condition of frustration in the cousin that, during a weekend in which all three of them drove to see a time-share in North Carolina that they were considering buying into, he lost all grasp of his sanity. The anger of all three had grown so great that they decided to buy a rifle as a quick and efficient means to bring about the end of their frustration. Back at the time-share, the cousin killed first the husband, then the wife, then shot himself, using his toe to push the trigger in the fashion made famous by Ernest Hemingway. Before committing this final act, the three of them visited the time-share office and invested their complete savings in one of the most expensive units in the resort. The wife's cousin had an estranged son who survived him, a son who hired a lawyer to see if he could reclaim the money squandered on the unused vacation property and perhaps sue the resort for additional damages, considering what he thought was their complicit responsibility in the deaths of his father and distant relatives. The lawyer (a personal friend who shared this story with us) determined that such a lawsuit would be fruitless, but he did get assurance from the resort that the son had free use of the time-share unit for all those times that his father had paid for, which included all major holiday weekends including Memorial Day, Labor Day, and Christmas.

AN ACCOMPLISHED RUNNER

A T THE MUNICIPAL POOL, I swam laps beside a woman who told me she had won her age group in the city marathon more than one dozen times. But, I soon learned as I watched her pull herself out of the pool, she had since lost control of her left leg, which dragged limply behind her. As we sat drying in the sun, reclined on plastic lounges, she explained to me that she injured her leg when she fell down a cellar hatch that gave under her weight as she was walking down the sidewalk. Her bones were broken so badly and her nerves damaged so severely that the leg had hung impotent ever since. The former marathon champion explained that she neither had any memory of the accident, nor did she remember the week following, and could only tell the story because she herself had been told it by one of the many witnesses. She admitted that her misfortune may have occurred because, on that day, she had become hyperaware of her stride, because the Sunday before she hadn't placed in the top ten in her age group in an organized race for the first time in a decade. As a result, she'd feared that her form had become flawed. She offered me advice I was never able to abide by in my search for my missing sister: a runner (she had decided) must never consider her pace or question her step; she must only move forward.

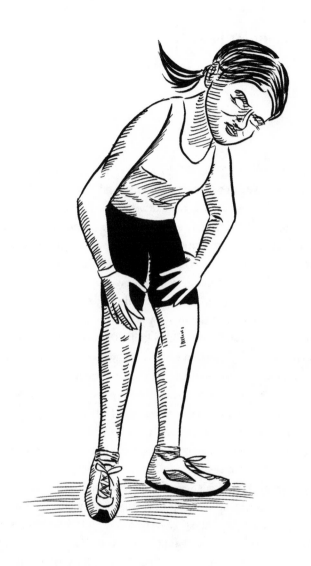

RIGHT TIME, RIGHT PLACE

Q UICK THINKING AND BRAVERY characterize the actions of a man in Waverly who saved two women from a drug-addled, would-be mugger, according to an article we read in the *Baltimore Sun*. The man, an appraiser for Legg Mason, a stalwart presence in Baltimore's economy that provides a substantial percentage of the city's employment and a great deal of support for the city's infrastructure, is reported to have distracted the attacker by offering him his Rolex watch if he let the women go. The women ran and escaped while the mugger reached for the watch, but, when the real estate appraiser tried to push the man away and run himself, the panicked mugger slashed him several times with a knife, then ran away without taking the watch, leaving the man to die on the sidewalk before the emergency responders arrived. The *Sun* reported that the man had just been setting his watch, which he received as a sixtieth birthday present from his four children, when the strung-out attacker approached the two women. At the real estate appraiser's funeral, his large family, his colleagues (including members of Legg Mason's upper management), as well as several civic leaders, dozens of people who had seen his story on the evening news, and even a representative from the Orioles were all in attendance. The next Sunday, the *Sun* ran an extended feature about the man, the incident, and the arrest of his killer. Accompanying the story were several full-color photos: one, taken at his graveside, of the two women who were saved; one of his four grown children standing together on a beach the previous summer; one of the bloodstained Rolex watch; one of the site of the murder, cordoned off with yellow police tape; and a mug shot showing the tired and haggard man who committed the crime. The accused, a legal expert suggested in the article, would, in all likelihood, never be released from jail.

A FORMER MAN OF INFLUENCE

E VEN THOSE WHO EFFECT SOME SORT OF INFRASTRUCTURAL CHANGE or score a particular systemic victory in Baltimore are not necessarily rewarded with respect, or even modest gratitude. For instance, a former city councilman, whose brother had been mayor and who would always have a place in the city's history for pushing through the project to reroute the highways away from densely populated areas, retired to his modest estate in Timonium and submitted himself to a kind of self-imposed house arrest, having food and other necessities delivered and never even going so far as to step into either his front or backyard. Therefore, no one was surprised that he had been dead for more than a week when his body was found by a delivery boy from the local pharmacy. He had subjected himself to one final punishment: death by hanging. He hanged himself in his den, in front of his oversized television, the screen of which displayed a paused image from Martin Scorsese's *Goodfellas* showing Joe Pesci playing the dead body of his character. The former councilman left a note asking his relatives to preserve his home as a monument to his isolation, and to leave his properly preserved body to rest in it alone, behind locked doors. This request was, of course, neither financially nor legally feasible, so they gave him a quiet burial at the local cemetery and sold his home for well below the market norm because of the sordid story surrounding its availability.

17

OLLOWING OUR DISAPPOINTMENT at the warehouse, obituaries became my only solace. They arrived faithfully on my doorstep each day and offered an itinerary of losses that temporarily distracted me from my own (loss of cause, loss of mission, loss of direction, loss of sister, and so on). For the first time, I began to understand what people had been telling me—not just me, but me and my companion—for so long, ever since we first met Lucia. I came to understand that I had designed a quest for myself that by its own definition could not come to a conclusion, could not be satisfied with answers, could only create further questions, whether I found my sister or not (or, perhaps, had already found her). This new understanding left me stranded in a strange city, alone.

My companion had left absolutely this time, leaving no trace, unlike the residue of his presence that remained during his first escape. I no longer found stained coffee cups in the sink or dirty shoes sitting in the vestibule. There were no damp towels hanging in the restroom, and the level of the whiskey bottle only dropped when I drank from it. Most importantly, no one ever took the morning paper off the front stoop before I did, no matter how late in the morning I rose. He had cleaned out his closet and collected his things. Not only was there no evidence of his presence, but there was also no evidence that he had ever been in that house, his uncle's house in Baltimore. I considered if he had left me because I had become an impediment to his search, or because he had abandoned his search and found it unnecessary to remain in the city that had claimed his brother. I certainly could understand and sympathize with either reason.

Looking back at that time, I had ended my search, but I didn't have the clarity and perspective to realize that. The interviews and research that had so recently consumed me seemed like impossible tasks. There were places I knew I could visit, and people I could talk to if I wanted to find the scent of my sister, but I couldn't bring myself to do either of those things. Instead, I read obituaries, lost myself in the voyeurism of others' emptiness, and allowed anyone's loss but my own to define my days.

I began each day by waking, walking to the front door to pull the daily edition of the *Sun* inside, then immediately returning to the warmth and softness of my bed. Once there, I read the obituaries section in its entirety, always keeping a ballpoint pen on my nightstand so I might make notes on details that intrigued me. I would begin with those items that warranted short articles and a photograph, typically corporate executives, local politicians, and those unreasonably involved in community groups. Then I would read those entries that had been submitted by family members directly (usually little more than a record of the deceased's occupation and a list of surviving relations), and finally I would look at the complete list of "death notices," minimal acknowledgements of passing lives reserved, I believed, for the lonely and the indigent.

I would often fall asleep reading about these deaths, and when I woke again, it would be late morning. Each day I would choose one or two obituaries, usually chosen from those lower on the list, that I hoped to learn more about. I would spend the rest of my day investigating the context around these deaths, the ramifications of each person's passing. Typically this would include a visit to a place of worship and a funeral home, and even private homes whenever the memorial gathering to fete the deceased was especially large, so I could attend the festivities unnoticed. Other times, I would visit the loved ones under the pretense of unrelated business, as a fire inspector or even an old friend of the deceased, and pretend to be ignorant of their recent losses, as this offered me the opportunity to observe their mourning in a painfully intimate way. I was there to study the survival techniques of those who had just experienced permanent loss, searching for examples of letting go, hoping to find a model for whatever my next step should be.

This routine I created became, unsurprisingly, a stalled and fruitless effort. The repetitive nature of the practice, which depended so essentially on beginning afresh each day with the delivery of the newspaper, ensured that, like so many of my personal undertakings, no ultimate progress could be made. This came to my attention one afternoon when I sat on the rear deck of a house in Highlandtown, where an Irish American family and their friends drank and laughed and mourned the death of a middle-aged man, a father of almost-grown children and a recently retired police officer. As I sipped my drink and enjoyed the early spring chill, a woman, pretty and tired looking, came outside to smoke a cigarette. I nodded, as I had learned to do, and looked out into the dusk settling over the neighborhood.

"How'd you know my dad?" she asked.

People almost never asked, so, when I attended these events, I didn't prepare a cover story. I was about to claim I had been a police force colleague, but quickly realized the complexity of that fiction, so I stammered, "From church. Knew him from church."

She nodded and blew out a mouthful of smoke. "So is it helping?" She waved her hand in the air. "All of this? Helping you process?"

"Well," I said, "he was a good man."

She laughed. "I'll give you that. But this—the toasts, the storytelling, the prayers, the goddamn bagpipes—isn't doing shit for me."

I smiled and shook my head, trying to maintain my anonymity as much as one could in a private conversation.

She flicked her cigarette and turned to go back inside. She smiled at me. "You didn't know him. You don't know anyone here. My brother saw you come in and was going to send you right back out. I told him not to. My dad would've poured you a drink. He liked sadness, enjoyed sharing it with other people. It's how he found meaning, I guess."

I was stunned. How often had people understood that I didn't belong at their events? I felt the need to defend myself. "I suppose you could say I didn't know him well."

"By 'well,' you mean, 'at all.'" She laughed again. "Here's the thing: I understand why someone would come to something like this. I don't think you're sick or crazy. There's something vital about these moments, about those who are living right after a death."

I nodded. She did understand.

"But, let me give you some unasked-for advice: Stop doing it. Not because it's disrespectful to the mourners; they want all the commiseration they can get. Don't do it because you'll lose yourself in it. It's too easy to define yourself by death and loss. You don't have your own raw materials, so you're using someone else's."

She understood exactly, more than I did myself. She lifted her drink and tapped it against my own. "Cheers," she said, and returned to the house. I was humiliated by our conversation, not so much because she'd detected my ruse, but because of the truth she exposed, the lack of learning that my deathwatches represented. I left their home immediately through the backyard and exited into a rear alley. I couldn't stand to have the woman and her family, who knew me for my weakness, look at me and expect me to look back at them. I took a bus home, and while I sat on one of its hard plastic seats and watched passengers get on and off, I felt the exhaustion from my months in Baltimore seize me. My fatigue froze me in place. The only thing that drew me out of the bus that evening was the promise of another drink.

PRO BONO

A WELL-RESPECTED SURGEON at the university hospital—who had received many civic recognitions for the pro bono work he did organizing emergency triage units in the more crime-ridden areas of the city, and who, after a long day treating the severely wounded, abandoned a family with two young children in the backseat of their car, a car which he had forced off the highway when he fell asleep at the wheel of his own sedan—excused his behavior to his wife by telling her that he had *nothing left to give.* While the doctor himself and the mother of the children survived the accident uninjured, the father and the two children didn't survive. Learning of this man's negligence caused my companion to consider that perhaps our siblings hadn't disappeared due to a heinous crime, but as a result of some person's gross sin of omission.

CROSSING SAFELY

A SCHOOL CROSSING GUARD in Towson lost her job after a child was struck and killed by a car driving through the busy intersection, which she was entrusted to by police. She hadn't helped the boy cross because, as she later admitted and several students who walked by her each day confirmed, she found it impossible to assist those children whom she thought were ugly. Weeks after the incident, she was committed to a psychological rehab center because of severe depression. Whether her sadness was caused by the boy's death or the loss of her job, which she claimed to have loved, is unclear. As a coping mechanism, she has taken to conducting pedestrian traffic in the center's courtyard, and the therapists allow her to direct the paths of her fellow patients. Her sister, who brought her to the rehab center, said that while they were packing for her stay, the former crossing guard insisted that she bring her bright orange sash, without which she would have *no self-respect*.

AT THE DEAD ANIMAL LENDING LIBRARY

M Y LEAST FAVORITE CIVIC INSTITUTIONS, which, to my knowledge, only exist in Baltimore, are dead animal lending libraries and, as such, I've always had a distaste for the people who frequent and work at these institutions. Yet, one afternoon, I visited the Baltimore Dead Animal Lending Library's Central Branch at the insistence of my friend, a psychotherapist, who claimed that this particular library was exceptional and more humane than other such libraries. My friend, who was my new neighbor, took me directly to the large rodent section and suggested that we borrow the skulls of three possums, which I agreed to. We asked the librarian for the three skulls and she graciously retrieved them for us and placed them in the middle of one of the many large viewing tables that were made available for the study of dead animals. My friend pulled a telescoping pointer from his pocket and began to poke and prod the three possum skulls in various places. Then, after several minutes of such irritation, one louse, followed by several more, crawled out from the interior regions of the skulls. The psychotherapist and I were so shocked by those living insects that we exited the building, nearly running down the hallways, having neglected to return the loaned possum skulls.

PARENTAL PIETY

WHILE MY COMPANION AND I had both had family members taken from us as children, a phenomenon we found particularly difficult to explain was how people sometimes choose to remove themselves from their families, no matter how dedicated those people might seem. Jim McNamara, the father of three teenage girls—all of whom ignored his requests for obedience, flouted his curfews, and claimed he didn't provide for them in a way they felt proper—never returned from a weekend trip he had taken. He went to Hilton Head, South Carolina, planning for three days of golfing, but, in fact, only made it to the hotel room overlooking the first course he had planned to play. This is where, on his first night, while taking a bath, he slit his wrists with razor blades purchased from a hobby shop. He died. In the top drawer of the metal desk in his study back home, a will was found, leaving his considerable wealth not to his devoted wife, but to his daughters. On top of his desk, laid neatly in the center of a blotter, was a note in which he begged the girls not to shoulder any of the blame for his death. He loved them. In fact, he was so frustrated by his failure to impress his love on them that he could not bear to attempt to show his love to them any longer. Despite his final action, he hoped that all three of them would understand him, his love, and, most of all, his myriad failures.

MISCARRIAGE

DESPITE THE FACT THAT my friend had miscarried her second child, the hospital continued to send her informational literature about infant development appropriate to the child's presumed age, as if the baby had grown to full term and been born. The hospital overlooked the fact that not a single one of its doctors had helped my friend deliver her second child.

PILGRIMAGE

M Y DISTANT COUSIN, who was also living in Baltimore, had a boyfriend, the owner of a failing coffee shop, who, by marrying my cousin, stood to come into quite a bit of money, as my cousin's father, my distant uncle, was a successful attorney in New York City. They did marry, in a small ceremony, and a few weeks later, the new husband announced that he was going to close up his coffee shop and start an arts nonprofit to support the city's youth, but he'd have to go on a trip to observe similar programs in other cities before he could "get the ball rolling." He estimated that a thorough study would take six months of travel, if not a year, and this time would allow him to create an organization more efficient than any similar ones, one that would produce remarkable results in the quality of life for the next generation of Baltimore's youth. He left, and, after a month, his daily phone calls to his new bride ceased. After six months, she was convinced she would neither see nor hear from him again. She reasoned that he had started a new life and suspected that charity work wasn't part of it. She did receive a phone call one night, from a police officer in Reno, Nevada. Her husband's bloodstained clothing had been found in an apartment he had rented on a weekly basis. The clothes were found on the same night that a shooting had been reported in his complex. The man had not been found, and, several months later, he was presumed murdered, but active pursuit of his killer was abandoned because of lack of evidence. My cousin found his death a relief, but she still had to care for his toddler son, the product of an earlier affair and a permanent reminder of my cousin's nuptial misstep. Almost a decade later, during my time in Baltimore, she saw a curious segment on *Entertainment Tonight,* which she watched most weekday evenings, about the tragic death of an up-and-coming Hollywood talent agent (he had drowned in the gentle waves off one of his client's private beaches), whom my cousin identified as her husband from the montage of close-up photos of him at nightclubs and movie premieres that flashed across her television screen. He had been living in California, using his legal name with a "Le" added before his surname. Judging from the abundance of cars, properties, and artworks that he had accumulated, my distant cousin realized that his wealth must have been even greater than hers, and she immediately hired a trusted local law firm to represent her in claiming his complete estate to care for her stepdaughter, his offspring. I found it bitterly amusing that while some people pined for children they had lost, others were cursed with more than they had hoped for.

18

I stopped pulling the newspapers off the front stoop and would simply let them collect until trash day, when I would deposit them directly into the bin that I had set out by the curb. Instead of reading the obituaries, I slept. I spent a lot more time drinking, which led to a lot more sleeping. It was usually early afternoon hunger that drew me out of bed, and an empty kitchen that drew me into the daylight. By the time I made it out, I was ravenous with hunger, and I wanted fried foods and sugar. I wanted beef and cheese and food soaked in oil or bathed in butter. I wanted pasta and milkshakes and slabs of cake from the diner on the corner. But even after eating these large meals, I wasn't satisfied. I always returned home still hungry.

By dinner, I usually felt slightly ill—not acute nausea, but the energy-draining properties of whatever gluttony I had committed at lunchtime. As such, I was disgusted by the thought of eating more, and, as such, I replaced my evening meal with courses of cocktails. This, in turn, led to a steady cycle of hunger and drunkenness and hangover and fatigue and pathological dissatisfaction, all of these states feeding each other. I also found that my ill-fated search for my sister and my failed career as a funeral tourist had not cured my vigorous appetite for schadenfreude as they should have. So I spent long evenings in bars, often from the thick of happy hour (blessedly a peaceful and affordable time to drink at most establishments) until the bartender asked me if I'd like one more as he or she mopped the floor behind the bar. I would always go to either a bar I had never been to or one I had visited rarely, not so much from a desire to be left alone, but a desire to be unknown. I actually sought conversation as I drank, but I never wanted to be the focus of that discussion. I preferred to listen rather than speak, which is fortunate, as the preponderance of bar patrons, in Baltimore or any city, prefer to share their own stories rather than listen to yours, and I was only too happy to oblige, assuming of course their stories were based on one or more key tragedies, which, being stories told to a stranger at a bar, they almost always were.

One evening, for more than an hour, a man and I sat drinking at a quiet bar with two empty stools between us. Surely we acknowledged each other with the occasional friendly nod, maybe shared banter with the bartender, but we hadn't spoken to each other. His face didn't look familiar to me, but I did notice that most of the patrons who walked by him paused for a moment and whispered something to their companions, if they were not alone. I also noticed the bartender lean in and say something to him conspiratorially, with a grin on his face, and I saw the man return a tired nod of politeness, suggesting that this attention was something he was accustomed to. He was obviously either a minor television celebrity or the subject of an extended and complicated news story that had passed probably a few years previously. I thought to ask him this, but predicted that while he seemed polite enough to answer, it would likely lead to a short and uninteresting conversation. The way the man sipped his drink and stared forward, I could tell he was hurting, and, from my experience, people who chose to experience this kind of pain along a bar rail rather than in the privacy of their own kitchens or bedrooms wanted to share their hurt with another as a way of easing it, but, I understood, a man such as this would have no interest in sharing his pain with a fan or a gawker. Instead, I offered him some folksy and sympathetic sentiment, something like "Long goddamn day, isn't it?" or "Another drink seems right just about now, doesn't it?" In my experience, these statements drew people to me.

He nodded and finished his drink. He looked into the empty glass and questioned whether he had had enough. In response, I drained my own and looked to the bartender, creating the suggestion that another one was in order. The man down the bar also raised a finger. I had seen what he was drinking, Irish whiskey with a single cube of ice, and I ordered it for him with my own drink.

"Thank you," he said, genuinely and pleasantly surprised, as they always were. "First good thing to happen all day."

"Figured as much. Rough one?"

"You could say that, but you'd be underestimating."

I laughed and thanked the bartender as he placed our drinks before us. I let the silence swell as we took one sip and then another.

"I thought I had a kid, but it turns out I don't."

I was seized for a moment with the fear that I had run into yet another person who had lost a loved one to abduction, but, in fact, his was a case of mistaken paternity, a case played out on a scale so grand that I would have dismissed the story as melodrama, had he not so convincingly related his experience to me.

"I never wanted a kid. I can't tell you that," he said. "So it's funny that I should be sitting here crying into my drink about not having a kid."

Part of the comfort I took in experiencing the struggles of others was the inevitable guilt they felt in publicly exhibiting suffering. Eventually, while they shared their stories, they apologized for the basic emotion that made the stories worth telling.

"But, ten years ago, when a woman told me I had a two-year-old child, who was I to say I didn't? I had, after all, committed the essential act at the appropriate time to make that child a reality."

I had spent so much time among those who defined themselves by the loss of a child that it almost offended me that anyone could see the possession of a child as an impediment to happiness.

"And I did the right thing. I didn't just send checks for the kid—I raised him. I helped raised him, at least. I'll give his mother that: she takes care of him. Then, a few months back, she's getting married—and good for her— starting a new chapter and all that, and she lets me know that my kid's not my kid. I didn't believe her, although it was certainly possible."

At that point the story felt more familiar, one I was accustomed to understanding.

"And, just today, modern science informed me that she's not lying. My child is someone else's child. I got what I always wanted."

I shook my head and raised my eyebrows and ordered us one more round, the most comforting gesture I knew. Offering an analysis of his tale, or a personal experience as a means of comparative sympathy, always failed. It was best to acknowledge the pain with a nod and a drink.

"Thanks," he said. "I'll be right back. Going to hit the head."

I sipped my next drink and experienced the particular warmth I felt after hearing another's story back in those days, the only moment, I am ashamed to admit, that I ever felt satisfied during that dark period.

A few minutes later, the man returned and sat beside me. "Hey," he said, "is your name Barney?"

I told him it was.

"Then this is for you." He handed me a neatly folded piece of paper with my name scrawled on it.

I unfolded the paper to find a photocopy of a parks department map, a map of the exact park where my sister had gone missing. The bank of trees where she was last seen (and where I had last seen Lucia) was circled, and written inside the circle was a specific date and time, one week subsequent.

"Where did you find this?"

"A woman gave it to me back there by the restrooms."

I looked to the back of the bar—it was vacant.

"She stopped me and asked if I could give this to you. I said she ought to come right up to you, but she didn't want to. Strange."

"Who was she?"

"I didn't get a name. Pretty lady. This might sound funny, but she looked a little like you. But prettier, of course." He laughed. "You have a sister or something?"

"I might," I said, and looked around the bar to see a trace of whomever it was he met. But it was just us and the bartender and the same two old men watching baseball in the corner and a few young professionals at the tables just beginning to become loud with drink.

The man sipped his drink and said, "Well, we all have our problems, don't we?"

I agreed wholeheartedly and stood up, leaving my glass half drunk on the bar, something I hadn't done in a very long time. I excused myself, wished the man the best of luck with his new situation, and went home immediately. For the first time in a very long time I had work to do, and I would need rest if I hoped to accomplish anything.

THE STALLION

MANY YEARS AGO, just before she was married, my distant cousin asked her neighbor to refurbish and customize a car, which she later gave to her husband on their wedding day. It was lavishly outfitted with a top-rate sound system, leather interiors, and horsepower more appropriate for competitive racing than street driving. My aunt (my mother's sister) and the rest of my cousin's family thought that her gift was sinfully extravagant, as she could have bought a modest home or four years of college education for her new stepdaughter for the price of the custom car. Almost immediately after the wedding, her husband left town in his car for an extended trip, and when the car was found abandoned after his supposed death in Reno, Nevada, it had been destroyed, the interiors torn apart and the engine and exterior accoutrements stripped from it. The one feature that was salvaged was the car's hood, with a hand-painted stallion adorning it. This was shipped to my distant cousin, who at that time was considered his widow. She had no interest in creating any sort of monument to her short-lived marriage. She created a lean-to in the back of her small yard with the car's hood, as a place to store her gardening tools. She of course laid the hood so that the underside was facing out, and the image of the stallion was hidden from view.

THE MOUTHY DRUNK

A FORMER STEAMFITTER, more recently know as a "nutjob" or a "mouthy drunk," who lived in the attic apartment of a row house he owned in Hampden, was found dying on the floor of his kitchen by an exterminator who was inspecting the roof for rodent holes when, through the window, he spied the old man's foot twitching. The retired steamfitter had been fetching himself a glass of water when he collapsed from a stroke, and, it was determined, he had lain on the dirty linoleum floor for three days, despite the fact that both his son and his daughter and their families lived in the house's lower-floor apartments. They avoided their father at all costs because of his alcoholism and general distemper. While lying on the floor, he managed to crack open his refrigerator and retrieve two apples and a pear that must have been at least two months old, and managed to eat several bites of the rancid fruit. The exterminator phoned for medical help immediately, but he had found the man much too late; he died that night in the hospital. His son and daughter and their families refused to visit him even on his deathbed, and the public response was that they should be charged criminally for their negligence. But his neighbors said they were justified in forsaking him, as he was the vilest man they had ever known, his mouth producing only curses and swears, and his eyes filled only with hate.

POSTPRANDIAL

A T A MIDDLE EASTERN RESTAURANT In Mount Vernon, a dinner was held in honor of a retiring school superintendent. The dinner attracted almost two hundred of his colleagues and friends (and friends' friends, including us), who spent most of the evening celebrating the passing of the schools' new budget, which the retiring superintendent had helped pitch to city hall. When the restaurant closed, several cars were called to shuttle the revelers home to various parts of the city, and, though we were at the front of the line, we stepped back to allow another group to take the first car, as the night was warm and I had carried half a glass of scotch outside with me and wanted to finish it. Right after the first car pulled away, it came to a halt, almost unnoticed by the rest of us. This was followed by the flash and booms of gunshots, which, obviously, we all did notice. A gunman dressed in black ran from beside the car and we all stood frozen beneath the restaurant's awning. Delayed screams coming from within the car caused us to move, but we were at a loss as to how we should respond. We all retreated back inside the Middle Eastern restaurant, where a vacuum hummed and buzzed. We stood inside the darkened restaurant, barely risking even a glance out the windows, until responding police officers came inside and revealed that three of the six people in the car had been killed in the robbery, but that they had secured the area, so it was safe to step outside. I have been forced to ask myself why I had decided to enjoy the end of my drink on the sidewalk and allow my friends to take the first car. Unfortunately, since that night, it appears from news reports that carjackings in Baltimore have only become more frequent.

19

O N THE STIPULATED DAY, I arrived at the park, at the exact time and no sooner, unlike most people who would arrive cautiously early for an appointment that they had invested with such import. But, on that day, I felt that arriving early seemed like a breach of some social contract that I had agreed on with whoever had summoned me, that we had a ritual to follow, almost as if this encounter were the culmination of a sacramental undertaking. So, at the very minute written on the note, I arrived at the exact place circled on the photocopied map that I had received, just where the vastness of the open grass met the shade and darkness of the woods. I stood there patiently, not speculating about what was about to occur, and certainly not questioning that something was indeed about to happen.

The week leading up to that moment in the park, the time I had spent since receiving the map from the man beside me at the bar, was marked by clarity and purpose. Those days were spent in preparation, allowing my mind and body to recover from the exhaustion they had been subjected to for so long. I slept regularly, ate well, and drank moderately. I spent most of the days taking long walks and reviewing the stacks of evidence my former companion and I had assembled, and not simply the documents and testimonials we had gathered since coming to Baltimore, but all those notes and records we had collected since we first met in the high school biology laboratory. During my walks, I recounted those incidents I had witnessed and those stories that I had been told to understand the depth of horrific experience that surrounded me. Doing so made me feel not only prepared, but also enthused to plumb the depths of horror that surround the revelation of truth. Although I had never admitted it, even to myself, for years I'd lived in fear of finding my sister, and my search thus coming to an end. I prepared to go to the park by confronting this exact fear, thereby overcoming any doubts that might hamper me.

On that day, I did not stray from routine, out of fear that doing so would create undue and problematic anxiety concerning my appointment. I drank coffee, brushed my teeth, and even watched the local news. Then, in the late morning, I boarded a bus that took me across town to the park, even though I understood that Baltimore buses, as in many cities, were the least reliable form of transportation, public or otherwise, and there was a distinct risk of delays. Still, I boarded a bus that would get me there on time, not early, as, that day, I had absolute and baseless faith in the reliability of the Baltimore Department of Transportation. And, in fact, I arrived at my destination promptly.

I entered the park, the note I received at the bar clutched tightly in my fist, because, now I realize, I felt it was some kind of ticket. The park was almost empty that day, as the air was unseasonably cold and the sky overcast. A drizzle had even begun to fall, which allowed me to cross the wide lawn of the park unimpeded by errant Frisbees, fetching dogs, and badly thrown footballs. The silence and vacancy of the park that day seemed to honor the sacred nature of my visit. I arrived at the place where I had last seen my sister, and the rain subsided so I could stand comfortably and wait for whoever this woman was who had promised to appear, or whatever other experience awaited me.

The next person to appear in the park was a young father pushing a baby carriage. I understood that young parents were slaves to whatever baby-calming ploys they developed to broker tenuous peace in their homes, and so would adhere to these techniques whatever the challenge, including inclement weather. I watched the man stride along the park's perimeter, having found a rhythm to soothe his child (including a regular stutter step, it appeared), any deviation from which he surely feared would wake the baby. I admired how absorbed he was by his mission, and I could not help to wonder if his child, like so many others, would be taken from him. I hoped this would never happen. He followed the park's edge and moved along the tree line, approaching me. I stepped back, allowing him to pass unimpeded, and when he did, he offered me a smile and a nod. That's when I noticed that his carriage was empty. He was trying to calm an absent child. The very thing I feared for this young father had already happened. He continued to follow the circuit around the park and exited back out the gate through which he had entered.

I continued to wait as I had been asked to, but minutes and then an hour passed, and no one arrived. Occasionally a person walked through the park, hurrying to avoid what looked like an approaching storm. That storm did arrive, and sheets of rain fell on the park. I stepped beneath trees for shelter, and even the thick covering of leaves soon gave way to the pouring rain, so I simply allowed myself to be soaked. The storm passed on, but the clouds and their grayness remained. Although I was thoroughly wet, I continued my vigil, waiting for the unknown woman. Hours later, the grayness turned to darkness as the sun set, and only then did I have to relent and admit to myself that I would be alone for as long as I chose to remain there. Just before the lights in the park reached their full brightness, I stepped away from the place I had been anchored to for so many hours, and hoped that I would not have to wait very long for the bus heading home.

THE DISSEMINATION OF SEATING

A FURNITURE MAKER who signed a contract with a dealer who ran a storefront in Ellicott City agreed to make dozens of chairs for several thousand dollars. He made a conscious choice to never visit the store and moreover never meet the people who bought his chairs, which had gained quite a reputation, and, even as demand, price, and sales increased over several years, he was able to maintain his distance. He had turned down no less than twenty invitations to wine and cheese socials and Sunday open houses that the furniture dealer organized at his store, and the furniture maker regularly threw away presumed thank-you cards without even opening the envelopes. The only thing he hated more than talentless salesmen who marketed "hand-crafted" and "antique replica" wares were the coarse egotists who bought them. So it came as a shock when, unannounced, he visited the dealer's booth at an open-air flea market one Saturday. The market was held annually and was considered the best sales opportunity of the year. The craftsman did not show until its closing hour, when most of the vendors had already begun to pack up their remaining merchandise. Once he had seen the lines for the concessions at the market, and realized that the same people who were buying six-dollar tacos were buying his chairs, he visited his dealer and informed him that he would no longer allow him to sell his pieces (despite the exclusive contract they had signed). A week later, he visited the store in Ellicott City with a list of further demands, which he read aloud on a busy Saturday afternoon. He demanded that the dealer return all profits he had made off the chairs, and that he recall all the chairs sold, so that they might be resold by the furniture maker himself, to sit in homes where they were properly appreciated. He refused to leave the store until his demands were met, so it became necessary for the dealer to contact the local police to settle the matter. While most people dismissed his demands as unreasonable (including the Baltimore Police Department), I admired the furniture maker for his dedication to a singular mission, and was inspired to maintain my own.

A NEW CONUNDRUM FOR THE STATE

A STATE CONGRESSMAN from Baltimore County conducted a small tour of local television and radio talk shows, giving interviews and discussing the steady increase of drug abuse among teens living in his district, a region characterized by economic privilege. The popularity of methamphetamine and illegally prescribed drugs belied the idea that drug abuse is primarily the domain of the poor. His statistics, which many questioned, claimed that per capita drug-related deaths were higher in his district than any other in the county. Based on this fact, he determined that drug abuse might be connected to freedom: freedom to be comfortable and unencumbered, rather than the pressure of constraint. He made the argument that the drug problem in his district must be addressed with state-funded programming, education, and counseling, just as it was in the inner city. The larger question the state congressman (who was a particular opponent of the governor's politics) was asking, citing the tragic death of the grandson of a local spice magnate, was, are we forgetting the plight of many of our citizens, simply because they have been damned with fiscal health?

HALF A PAIR OF JORDANS

A SINGLE AIR JORDAN SNEAKER that was found on the front patio of a house in Greenmount has done little to help clear up a missing person case that began the summer we were in Baltimore. The sneaker unquestionably belonged to Bonneville Stanton, who had been a salesman at the local Foot Locker. Stanton had been desperately sought by his estranged half sister, as he was the only person aware of her father's true identity, information that their mother shared with Bonneville at the end of her long bout with multiple sclerosis, which he promised not to share with his half sister until her twenty-fifth birthday, as her mother feared the influence the man might have on her daughter's life. Stanton was found dead in a wooded area in Druid Hill Park, where his body had apparently lain for just a few days. Where he had been since the summer is still a mystery. The last time he was seen alive, he had punched out of work at Foot Locker in the middle of a double shift and headed for Royal Farms to get some Ring Dings *for energy*. He never punched back in.

O
N THE DAY I STOOD IN THE RAIN and waited for a woman who never arrived, my faith was shaken, but I didn't abandon my revived search for my sister. In fact, the disappointment of that day simply bolstered my resolve and led to yet another daily routine, one that included a trip to the park with the full intention, on each given day, of meeting the woman who hadn't appeared on the first day. I spent whole days in that park; a place that once held such sublime power in my imagination became as familiar and regular to me as the pair of socks on my feet. Each day, on entering the park, I walked directly to the place that had been circled on the map, fully expecting to find someone waiting for me, as I felt that spot of earth owed me something, considering how much it had already taken. I would wait there and allow someone or something to reveal itself. Sometimes I would even sit on the soft ground.

The glimpse of hope that the photocopied map had given me, in fact, tapped into my most vicious instincts, reviving my interminable search once again and giving me a concrete reason not to abandon it as I should have. That map with its handwritten scrawl allowed me to ignore the understanding I had of the pathological nature of my undertaking, and the clear vision I had of the inevitable disappointment that would come from living a life defined by loss.

As I began my search again, the questioning and the investigations and unlikely fact-finding missions, I began to suffer from another loss: that of my longtime companion and fellow seeker, whose absence had been so long and complete and had admitted no suggestions of his continued existence whatsoever, that I could no longer deny I was alone. Perhaps that is why I returned to the park each day, as it provided that sliver of hope that, at that point in my life, I might not be completely alone.

Each day, when I approached the spot in the park, I found nothing, yet, on the one day when I did make a discovery, I felt no surprise at all, a testament either to my faith or delusion. I noticed a figure standing among the trees, not far from the spot that took my sister. I stared at the figure and it began to move, and soon I could tell that it was approaching me. From out of the trees stepped a woman, looking down and hiding her face from me, embarrassed like a child. She looked up and I saw Lucia's face, a wracked and tired version of her face, one that had aged considerably in the few short months since I had last seen it, the moment she had assured me and my companion that she would never return to Baltimore, an oath I never questioned. Standing before me, she seemed more flustered by my presence than I was by hers. She was unable to speak, so I offered a hand, which she accepted, and ushered her to a nearby bench, where we sat for a very long moment, watching children play on the bright spring afternoon.

"I didn't want to come back," she said.

I didn't doubt her claim, nor was I surprised that she couldn't stay true to her wishes. I'd experienced the same failure. "You came back because you had something to tell me."

She shook her head. "You're the last person—one of the last people—I hoped to find."

I looked back to the woods where she had stood. "So why were you . . . why did you wait? There?"

"Because," she said, "because I thought I would find him there."

"Thomas?" I breathed the name of my departed friend.

"No. My brother."

It hurt to ask, but I knew I had to. "And have you found him?"

"No," she said. "You should know by now. We can never find them. Not in the way we want to."

"So, I'm not . . ."

"Not him?"

"Yes, not him?"

"You were never him. You could never have been him."

"Why not?"

"Because there are facts, Barney. Facts of time and space. Incontrovertible truths of biography. And whatever systems we may feel but not understand, these operators are bound by the same limits. The details of my childhood and your sister's disappearance, and my brother's abduction, and your mother's existence, preclude the fact that you and I are brother and sister."

She reached into her coat and pulled out a frayed newspaper clipping. It showed a crying woman holding a photo of her son, one of those Little League portraits portraying a kneeling boy with a bat propping up his elbow. I scanned the article and the city and the date and the woman crying—none of these things could accommodate my conception of losing my sister.

"That's the exact article I showed him on the day we first met back in college."

"So he knew all along that you weren't my sister? So why did he insist?"

"Just because he had the facts doesn't mean he believed them. That story worked for him. It created a sense that answers existed. If you and I had found each other as brother and sister, it would prove the missing could be found."

"I see." I felt relief, but also desperation, sinking into a deeper hole in my stomach, entrenching itself.

"So you haven't found your sister. I'm not her. I can't be her."

"So why were you here today? Did you get a note?"

"Not today. But I've gotten notes and maps. I've run through empty warehouses and ridden buses to abandoned parts of town. I've left Baltimore only to receive mysterious phone calls and letters, enough to draw me back. I've even found my way to the hospital, and I've seen the paperwork to prove that my brother is there, or was there."

"The hospital?"

"All of it. I've done it all and found nothing."

We watched a boy run up to his father, who hugged him. They walked across the lawn to a car that was waiting on the street. The smiling pair got in and pulled away.

"So the only thing I can make sense of," she said, "is that I found you here today, and the only good I can do is to take you with me, out of this city."

I looked away. She had to understand that I wouldn't leave with her that day, or any day. I looked back at her. "Tell me about the hospital."

"One week ago," she said, "if you had found me, I would have given you what you wanted. I would have answered your questions, because I was desperate enough to believe that I was close to finding my brother and everyone else."

"But now you know better?"

"I do." She stood up, feeling me slip away from her, understanding that she did not have the means to help me. "I also know that you won't leave with me today."

"Just the name of the hospital."

"Don't worry, you'll end up there. It's just a matter of time." Then she walked away, and this time I believed, once again, that she would not return to Baltimore.

I sat on that bench until Lucia was out of sight, not long, as she walked quickly and with purpose. I left the park, resolved of very little except that I would not return the next day.

MISTAKEN IDENTIFICATION

L ATE ONE NIGHT, my companion and I walked home through the central part of the city after having enjoyed several cocktails at a patio bar beside the harbor. We were excited, as it was an unusually warm early spring evening. As we walked, we sang a song that had been popular the summer we first met, and that we had probably forgotten since then. The streets were almost empty in the central part of the city, as it was largely a financial district, but a young man, who looked to be about twenty-five years old, stood in the middle of the sidewalk directly ahead of us and called for our attention. We maintained our strides, dodging to either side of him, and continued without slowing down, anxious to get home and in bed, especially considering the fact that we were due to be at a picnic in Druid Hill Park before noon the next day. The picnic was a brunch held annually by a local widow to celebrate her late husband, an insurance executive who was killed doing relief work in Belize during an extended summer vacation. It was known as the most raucous memorial that people had ever experienced. As visitors to the city, we were honored just to be invited and did not want to arrive late. The man on the sidewalk spoke unintelligibly and grabbed my companion by the upper arm, but he couldn't maintain a grip for more than a moment. I looked back as we moved on, and I saw the man stumble, list to his left, then to his right, and ultimately fall to his knees, at which point he let forth a wail. In truth, we both avoided him out of fear that he was one of the many destitute homeless who were known to be involved in criminal acts of desperation. According to the newspaper, many of these people had been prematurely released from various detention centers and criminal rehabilitation clinics (as identified by contemporary euphemism). We imagined that he might beat us mercilessly—or worse.

The reality is that we would have shoved him to the ground and run right over his fallen body to avoid becoming his next victim, as we saw it. At the picnic brunch the next day, a day almost as mild as the one before it, the widow seemed glum, and it wasn't due to the memory of her late husband, a memory she meant to celebrate, but because she had been awoken by a phone call that morning, a call informing her that her nephew, a troubled but kind young man, had been found dead on the streets, having received two stab wounds to his stomach. The wounds didn't kill him immediately, but he continued to hemorrhage blood as he struggled to find help, and, by the time he was found, he had already died under the bright light of a streetlamp in the financial district. Considering our position as guests and newcomers, we made no mention of our encounter the night before and offered our kind hostess our most sincere condolences.

263 JOHN DERMOT WOODS

A HUSBAND AND WIFE

THE MARRIAGE OF A WELL-LOVED LOCAL COUPLE, which had begun when they were quite young, had grown strained as life pulled the husband and wife in separate directions. My companion and I had held both in the highest regard, and had admired their contrasting spirits since coming to town. The husband was a painter who could infuse sublime possibility into even completely mundane subjects, and the wife was a successful real estate broker whose systematic approach made obvious the most abstract reason behind the value of a particular property. As visits to their studio apartment became characterized more and more by their spiteful bickering, we visited the couple less and less. Eventually we learned indirectly, through other friends, that the couple had divorced after the wife had sold a reclaimed warehouse—one the husband saw as the perfect location for the studio-gallery of which he had always dreamed—to a real estate developer who planned to turn the warehouse into spacious loft apartments, not unlike the one the couple themselves lived in. Eventually the husband actually moved into one of the new lofts and, living alone inside of it, set to painting oversized canvases with a violent passion that he had never before exhibited. Likewise, the wife pursued her career with the same vigor, specializing in brokering the sale and resale of refurbished factories and warehouses beside the river. Still a young man, the painter was found dead in his loft one day, paintbrush in hand, having worked until the end. He was the victim of an undiagnosed blood disorder. Within the month, his ex-wife died as she stood alone inside a newly purchased warehouse and determined the most lucrative way to reoutfit the space. She had been diagnosed with a heart condition, but chose to take no measures to prevent the condition from proving itself fatal. As each had begun to recognize his and her respective goal, they found they could no longer tolerate sharing in a union. But it was perhaps the dissolution of this partnership that led to their hurried and unforeseen deaths. My companion and I took their deaths as an object lesson, considering that we had formed our own partnership through a singular goal of having lost something in the city of Baltimore and the desire to recover it.

ALL DAY, UNDERGROUND

ONE WEDNESDAY NIGHT, a weakened man—an electrician and father of three—was dragged off a train car that was stopped at the Charles Center station after he had sat in the car all day, riding it back and forth on the short subway line, never once standing, let alone eating or drinking. He explained that as he'd traveled into downtown by way of the rarely traveled Baltimore subway to go to work at the nearly completed Inner Harbor restaurant he was helping to build, he was struck with a sudden anxiety as to what purpose his life would have once the restaurant was complete. This concern bolted him to his seat, and, although he wished to stand up and get off every time the train car doors eased open, he sat still, stock upright, for more than twelve hours straight. To ease his anxiety, he repeated the names of the stops in order in his head, alternatively from north to south, then south to north. When he began to find this maddening, he instead spoke the name of the next stop each time the train doors closed. His wife retrieved him from St. Mary's Hospital, where he had been taken because of his dehydration and fatigue. He was on disability leave when the restaurant was finished, but it is unclear whether he ever returned to his work as an electrician.

THE LAST TIME I LEFT THE PARK, finally convinced that I would not find my sister where I had lost her, I did not take the bus home. Instead, I began to walk into the neighborhood beside the park, a neighborhood I knew nothing about. It was a steady and aimless amble, not meant as a stroll that would relax me by exposing me to the world around me, but as a kind of defensive motion, designed to hold off the deluge of regret that was sure to wash over me if I remained still, even for a moment.

That day highlighted the fact that Baltimore streets are often barren of people, and this seemed to be the case regardless of geography, economic or racial demographics, and, most compellingly, regardless of the time of day. The single exception was the downtown tourist district, an inorganic neighborhood created in the city's recent history near the harbor, the kind of place those living in a city generally avoided. But, on that day, I felt the draw of human company, or at least the presence of living bodies and the sounds of voices. The strangeness of this desire was apparent to me even at the time, as, like most people, I normally desired to be alone following times of abject disappointment, so I might be able to come to understand this disappointment rather than be asked to interpret it prematurely for the sake of others. Yet, on that day, I found the empty streets that I crossed hopelessly lonely. This might seem like an expected reaction to empty streets, but, during my time in Baltimore, empty streets (or buildings or parks) usually excited me, as they suggested the possibility of discovery rather than abandonment. That day, my feet carried me toward the voices I heard, but these were few and always fleeting. The streets would empty soon after I approached.

Eventually I discovered that the one place I could find the sustained company of others was on the benches down beside the harbor, so I positioned myself near the center of a nexus of attractions that included an aquarium, a shopping mall of restaurants, a ballpark, and a football stadium. I sat on a bench and knew that if I considered the events of the afternoon in the park (and the weeks that lead up to it [and the years that led to those weeks]), I would be paralyzed by failure. So, instead, I focused on the one detail that could move me forward: the hospital. I knew the hospital was where I must end up, but I didn't know when I would be prepared to visit it, and if I would know what to do once I got there. Moreover, I began to question if I would ever know, or if I could ever be prepared. This thought overwhelmed me so completely that I decided to do what I often decided to do at times such as those—I decided to get myself a drink.

I stood up from the bench and walked to the nearest bar, which was part of a larger restaurant that marketed itself primarily by touting the quality of its buffalo-style chicken wings and the tightness of its waitresses' T-shirts. The bar was long and half full, exactly the kind of place where one could drink and contemplate things while surrounded by the noise of humanity, yet undisturbed by the direct engagement of other people. I ordered a beer and the bartender suggested that the thriftier option would be to order a pitcher, so I did. Over the next few hours I enjoyed several watery pitchers of the house draught, enough to make me considerably drunk, despite the weakness of the beer.

The bartender was good enough to let me stay at the bar while she cleaned, so when I eventually emerged onto the plaza beside the harbor, the area was virtually empty, like the streets away from the center of town that I had walked through earlier in the day. Lights lit the area as if it were midday, but the dark buildings surrounding the plaza and the lack of chattering voices let me know that it was the middle of the night. I walked to the rail that ran along the harbor's edge, following it as I watched the fluorescent signs of the shuttered restaurants and stores reflecting off the black water. My drunkenness exposed my consciousness to the pitfalls of sadness and regret, so rather than consider how I might find and enter the hospital that, in all likelihood, housed my long-missing sister, I began to think about Lucia and the one chance I had to care about something I had as much as I cared about something that I had lost. I considered the second and third chances that she and the world had conspired to give me. I considered the permanence of her exit that afternoon, and the embarrassment I felt as I sat in that park by myself for those last few moments.

I became distracted by a sound coming from the water, a knock I heard once and then again and then again; soon, the knocks began to multiply, a hushed and persistent chorus. I stood on the pier and inspected the water beneath me to see what this sound was. I saw something, or some things, moving on the water below, so I bent down to get a closer look, to identify what was milling in the inky water, and as I did, I felt my balance abandon me, and, no longer sure whether my head was above my feet or my feet above my head, I felt the damp and cold of the water as it swallowed my body.

I saw blackness, then I saw lights. White and red and yellow and blue lights surrounded me.

22

WOKE BECAUSE THE MIDAFTERNOON SUNLIGHT had found its way through the slats of the blinds in my room and struck me in my closed eyes, filling my slumber with a red glow. It wasn't the first time I had awoken that day. I was awoken, although not quite as fully as I was by the afternoon light, sometime in the morning by someone I remember as a girl in a dress, who I now realize must have been a nurse or social worker or other hospital employee. It was hard for me to focus on what she told me, but I did recognize I was in a hospital, the same hospital, I assumed, that Lucia had mentioned.

Lying peacefully in the quiet room, I thought about what the girl, the woman, had told me. She said I had fallen in the water the night before, but officers on a patrol boat from the Baltimore Police Department's marine division had saved me. Apparently I was not as alone as I had thought, or felt, out on the plaza beside the harbor. My stroll along the water's edge was, in fact, a pronounced drunken stumble, and not only had a few passersby taken notice of me, but the police had as well. It seemed that place where I fell was a small dock beside a paddleboat rental, and the sound that had so interested me was simply the moored paddleboats knocking against each other, disturbed by the wake of the slowly approaching patrol boat, whose pilots wished only to check on my safety. And when my body did tip into the water, through a combination of shock and inebriation, I did a very bad job at keeping myself afloat, and, in fact, judging from my complete lack of recall, I failed to remain conscious at all. Fortunately, using a strong spotlight, the police officers were able to pull my wet body to safety with relative ease. Subsequently, they delivered me to this hospital to recover. I remembered the girl-woman beside my bed, telling me I would be able to leave just as soon as the doctors were confident I had suffered no ill effects from my dip in the cold water.

I felt relatively well lying in the bed, having had most of a night and a day to sleep and recover. I looked to see if I had any monitors or IVs or other apparatuses attached to my body—I did not, an indication of my health, I thought. I was now fully awake, and felt that it was contingent on me to simply do something, but I also felt some general obligation to wait for affirmation from a medical professional before I did. So I first lay in that bed, then I sat on its edge, then I stood beside it, then I pulled up the blinds and watched the parking lot below. All this time, no one came to see the hospital's sole survivor of drunk drowning. I expected that if not a doctor or a nurse, some staff member or maintenance worker would have occasion to open the door and visit my room, but, as the afternoon wore on, none did. In the quiet of the room, I could hear clicks and ticks and the muffled voices of nurses chattering in the hallway. As it turned toward evening, and no hospital meal was delivered, I soon realized that I was being left alone, that I had been delivered to the place where I might find my sister, and a rupture in the system that governed this institution had created a chance for me to pursue my search. I was wearing a hospital robe, which would serve not only to cover me, but also to make me appear as if I belonged in whatever part of the hospital I might explore. I put on the slippers that sat beside my bed and walked into the hallway.

Once there, I grew decidedly light-headed, so leaning against the wall provided a much-needed balancing aid. Otherwise, I felt healthy and strong. I smiled at the few hospital employees who passed, and none of them seemed to take any particular notice of me. I suspected I would not have my bed at the hospital for long, so I set about seeing what I might discover as quickly as possible. I checked a hospital directory posted on the wall and searched for pediatrics, thinking this would be the reasonable place to begin a search for missing children, and found that the pediatric unit was in the same wing of the hospital I was in, only two floors up. I walked immediately to the elevators.

On the way there, I heard the sound of laughing children coming from behind two solid doors, through which I could see nothing. I guessed it could have been a family visiting a loved one, or some kind of school trip, but the sounds of those children's voices in a place where children weren't meant to be drew me in. I pushed on the doors and they immediately swung open. Inside was a carpeted room full of institutional, multicolored tables at which children, none of whom appeared unwell, sat playing games and eating small snacks. Much like the cafeteria we had observed inside the warehouse, not a single adult was apparent in the room. I walked inside, but none of the children stopped to acknowledge me, so I sat at a table where one young boy was sitting, drinking a juice box and gnawing on a handful of traffic cone–orange crackers. As a sort of test, I reached into his pile of crackers and took a few, placing them in my mouth. The boy looked up at me and smiled, then returned to his drink box.

A group of children played checkers beside me; they were certainly animated in their reactions to the game, cheering and groaning as if playing a tennis match, but they remained unfailingly polite. In fact, the whole room of children operated with restraint and respect for each other, something rarely seen in the absence of adult supervision. I felt quite sure I had found the place in the hospital Lucia had referred to in the park.

After a few short minutes, I felt a tap on my shoulder. I turned to see an older man in a lab coat standing above me. I was afraid, remembering the roughness with which we were handled by the men inside the warehouse. Yet this man smiled and said, "Excuse me, sir, but I think you may have gotten lost."

I couldn't deny his claim.

"Just over that way is the place you're most likely trying to locate." He pointed back at the doors through which I'd entered.

He couldn't have been more inaccurate, but I was in no place to state this. Instead, I said, "Is this pediatrics?"

"No, sir," he said. "That's on the fourth floor." He pointed again at the door. "That way," he said, and placed a hand on my back.

I stood up, uninterested in any sort of conflict. I thought it'd be best to return to my room in peace, so I might still have another opportunity to investigate this strange room. He watched, smiling the whole time, and I left, returning to the security of my hospital room.

Inside I found the cleaning staff hard at work mopping the floor and stripping the bed of its sheets. They looked up at me with confusion. "Can I help you?" one of them asked.

"This is my room."

"Sorry, sir," she said. "Not yet. We're still cleaning."

"No," I said. "This has been my room. I've been staying here. I'm still staying here."

The other cleaner looked at a clipboard. "Last patient in this room was discharged this morning."

"That's not right."

They both shrugged and set back to cleaning. Only then did it occur to me that I might have, in fact, been discharged, and that I had somehow fallen asleep when I was collecting my things, and perhaps by some oversight I had been left in my room. I peered down the hall to where I had left the children behind the thick steel doors, and I watched the cleaners destroying any trace of my presence in their hospital, and looked down at my body, covered in a thin robe and cheap slippers, and saw myself for what I had become: a fool who'd given up everything to complete an impossible errand.

STILLNESS

O N A VISIT TO THE WEST VIRGINIA MOUNTAINS, one of our few trips outside of the city while we were living there, we met a lawyer, originally from Baltimore, who had lost his job at a large firm ("for ethical reasons," he said) in the city and opened a private practice in the rural town where we met him. We visited him at his office, hoping to learn about his experience of leaving the city to find answers, a solution that seemed increasingly attractive to us. We had learned about him when a gas station attendant in the town had told us about *the lawyer from Baltimore*. He was friendly, but exhausted looking, and, even though it was eleven o'clock on a Tuesday morning, he had a bottle of scotch in front of him, which he frequently tipped into his glass, the only other object on his large desk. He said he had made the mistake of granting an interview with the *Sun* in which he discussed the problems with the business of corporate law and certain opportunities for abuse of the system, which got him pushed out of his partner position at his firm and prevented him from being hired by any of their competitors. He accepted his fate and moved to that small town in West Virginia, a state he had never before visited, away from the strain and money of his former life. His family had found the stillness and loneliness of it unbearable, which further complicated his already tested marriage, and led his wife to leave him and take his two children back with her to Maryland. Without his family, the stillness and loneliness overcame the lawyer, but he couldn't leave the town, as he couldn't afford to move his practice, especially considering his professional ruin and the steep alimony and child support payments he had to pay each month. He insisted that it all went wrong when he accepted his first job as an associate at the law firm that eventually ruined him, first depriving him of a public life, then stealing his home life. He insisted that anybody who was willing to accept that much money from a corporate interest would, in some way, be destroyed by that institution. He admitted that even as recently as the morning that we met him, he had placed calls to the human resources departments of firms in the city, inquiring about open positions—not a single one of these calls had been returned (perhaps this was the reason for the scotch). He was quite sure the firm wished to kill him slowly with misery, despite that fact that he had always been an effective employee and had even wished to help the firm when he publicly criticized the system it was a part of. We sat across his desk from him, completely at a loss for even one word of consolation. On the day we were leaving, after a short morning hike, we ate lunch at the one coffee shop in town. Our waitress informed us that the lawyer had hanged himself the night before. The next week, in the back of the *Sun*, there was a memorial to the lawyer, a paid advertisement, dedicated not by his ex-wife or children, but by the law firm where he had worked for twenty-five years.

STAND-UP

THE STAND-UP COMEDIAN, who carried a cane in his left hand and had a left leg that did little more than drag behind his right, performed one night at a one-hundred-dollar-a-plate benefit for the Guilford Chamber of Commerce. We asked if he would like to join us at a house on the Eastern Shore that my companion and I had rented for the month of August, a house we planned to open to any entertainer who was willing to perform his craft (and we would happily provide him with home-cooked meals and a beach pass for the duration of his stay). He said he'd be delighted to come. We made a simple request of the stand-up comic (who was originally from Queens, New York, but had moved to Maryland after high school and had once sold bottled water outside the baseball stadium), and that was to present a new routine when we met again at the shore, to lampoon a completely different subject than he had for the Guilford Chamber of Commerce, although we did snort with laughter during his fundraiser performance. He said that wouldn't be a problem, and, in August on the Eastern Shore, he did, in fact, provide us with a completely new routine, skewering everyone from the newly elected mayor to the president of the chamber of commerce to the dairy industry for having given up the fight to locate missing children (the latter joke made us laugh the hardest). He invited us to offer our own targets of ridicule (naturally my companion and I suggested one another), and he hilariously roasted them as well. But when, toward the end of his performance, as evening turned to night, we asked that he address his tired left leg, he said he could not, as he was uncomfortable with physical humor.

MISTAKEN AGGRESSION

A FRIEND, ONE OF OUR FEW VISITORS from back home, was arrested while visiting us in Baltimore because a waitress at a popular Canton vegetarian restaurant accused him of calling her into the men's room (complaining that he had fallen) and then aggressively fondling her once she stepped inside. He dismissed the accusation as nonsense and called it "typical cosmopolitan xenophobia." This was a phenomenon my companion and I believed in, and we wondered if it was a contributing factor to our failed search for the brother and sister whom we had lost. Our friend was a fourth-grade teacher at a public school back home, and came to stay with us in Baltimore as an attempt to recover his senses after having taught a particularly petulant batch of nine-year-olds during the previous school year. But the drastic change of environment, and the noise and excitement of the city, only weakened him further, sending him into a deep depression that forced him to confine himself to our guest room for most of the day. We'd finally convinced him to leave the house for dinner that night, and it was necessary for my companion and I to each support one of his arms just to hold him upright as he walked. After the police arrested him, they quickly determined that he was incapable of fondling anyone aggressively, and allowed him to return to the restaurant to finish his dinner. The waitress was fired immediately, though no charges were filed, and after watching a news report about her disgrace on television the next morning, she drank a bottle of nail polish remover, either as an act of penance or as an attempt at taking her own life. Last we checked, she remained a patient recovering at the University of Maryland Medical Center, but doctors had determined that there was no chance she would ever speak again because of the severe damage to her throat.

23

WALKED HOME FROM THE HOSPITAL clothed in a thin cloth robe and slippers. I was too embarrassed to approach the nurse's station before leaving to ask about my clothes and other personal effects, as I had come to believe that I had been successfully discharged earlier in the day and simply returned to an empty room for a nap. Rather than dealing with the shame of discussing why I was still wandering the hospital halls (and trespassing on gatherings of children within, no less), I decided to bear the mild indignity of walking home in minimal paper clothing. I avoided the humiliation of riding a bus and walked across town instead, focused simply on returning to the house, where I would perhaps take a bath, certainly put on soft clothes, and hopefully be in bed shortly after sundown.

When I got to the familiar and barren house that was my home in Baltimore, I realized, for the first time, that I had no keys to let myself in. With no other options, I turned the knob on the front door; to my surprise, it opened. I couldn't imagine I had left it unlocked, as I never left the door to the Baltimore home unlocked, even when I ran to the corner store for a cup of coffee or a roll of toilet paper. I entered, expecting to find an intruder, but instead found a home that was completely undisturbed, left as quiet and settled as it had been when I left the previous afternoon. I walked through the front hallway and parlor and saw nothing askew. I stopped and listened for signs of another human, but I detected nothing. Then I stepped into the kitchen and saw a single piece of evidence that someone had visited the home: several sheets of paper on which a hand-scrawled letter had been written, lying atop the table. The sight of the letter made me forget my desire for comfort and rest when I recognized the hand of my absentee companion.

I paused for a moment to see if he was still in the house, perhaps standing over my shoulder—he was not. Still clothed in paper, I sat down in that dusk-darkened kitchen and read the letter with the last of what was left of the daylight.

The letter was both a confession and a farewell. Little of what he told me in the letter was new, as he recounted my own experiences of the last few weeks. The only surprise was his knowledge of these events. He had apparently been attendant for these moments, and, it seemed, instrumental in their occurrence. He wrote of the sadness he felt watching me day after day, bedraggled, stepping out to the stoop and pulling in the newspaper, clearly believing it contained the hope of personal salvation. He wrote of me attending the funeral of a young woman I had never met, and the strain on my face as I listened to the graveside words of a minister whose church I had never attended, and how I clearly expected more of those words than any of the sobbing mourners beside me did. He wrote of sitting in the shadows of the bars that I visited from the early evenings to late nights and palpably feeling my desire for human sustenance, and wanting to provide just that, as he had for so long, but ultimately insisting that he not reveal himself. He even wrote of my long and repetitive days in the park, and of following my progress from lawn to trees to bench. Then he revealed that he was also present when I found Lucia watching me. Not only that, but he had observed several other moments, including that night I received the note in the bar. He had seen her watching, constantly fighting to reveal herself, the same impulse he'd suppressed in relation to not only me but also to her.

Finally he wrote of the night by the harbor, when I fell into the dark water. That night, he wrote, was when he had the greatest hope, when he thought that his plans, or "our plans" as he called them, might be realized. He wrote of the straggling tourists running to the place where I had fallen, and the beauty of the patrol boat's flashing lights illuminating the otherwise black water below. He wrote of the fear and hope he felt as my body was pulled from the harbor, admitting that the fear and hope didn't pertain to whether I was dead or alive, which he truly didn't know, but to the fact that my accident was sure to precipitate an end to our long search. He also suggested that he took some responsibility (and credit) for my accident that night, and wasn't sure that he had fully prepared himself for the incident's outcome. He wrote of the sense of relief he felt when he saw the nurses outside my hospital room laughing and shaking their heads, confident that my tribulation wasn't life threatening. He also admitted to feeling deflated at that moment, understanding that this event was not the ultimate catalyst he'd hoped it would be. He even watched as I wandered the hospital hallways in hopeless pursuit of children's voices; it was then that he decided he would finally leave Baltimore. I can only assume that he returned to the chair in which I was sitting, wrote the note I was holding, then left.

He thought that if he observed events from a removed position, events such as my investigations and even the abduction of other children, he would gain an insight into his own search that he otherwise never would. But he confessed that this tactic was futile from the beginning, implicated as he was, and involved as he was since childhood. He could never expect any kind of objectivity or removal from the story of the missing children. And so, understanding this, he had left Baltimore, claiming, like many before him, never to return.

Having read his letter, and finding myself barely clothed in a dark and empty kitchen, no closer to my sister than I had been when I came to Baltimore, I realized my decision to leave had been made for some time, but I had been living the life of a zombie, driven by a hunger of which I had no understanding. I stood up from the table and drew myself a bath. I washed completely and dressed. I packed my belongings in a small bag and I left the house, resolved to never spend another dark night in the city that had already taken so much of me.

SISTER CITIES

WITH THE SUCCESS OF GOODWILL PROGRAMS set up between Baltimore and cities in Russia, China, and East Africa, the city government sent a representative to Indonesia to investigate which smaller cities on the main island of Java might serve as the newest of Baltimore's many sister cities. The representative, a recent college graduate who had majored in theology, left for Indonesia in early August, a particularly hot month in Southeast Asia. He called after arriving safely in Jakarta and said that he'd return in no more than a month with reports on at least five cities. Two months later, nothing had been heard from the young man; e-mails went unanswered, and the basically uncooperative Indonesian government said it had no evidence of any lost Americans within its borders. So another recent college graduate—this time a young woman—was sent to gather information about the whereabouts of (and hopefully locate) the missing representative. She too reported in after safely arriving in Jakarta, and called again from Bandung, the first city on the missing man's itinerary, to report that she had found no new information concerning his location. But her calls ceased after that, and for another month nothing was heard from her, which caused city hall to dispatch yet another rescuer. This time it was a retired university professor—he spoke Indonesian, had studied Indonesian urbanity, and had even lived in Jakarta for many years. This second rescuer, however, despite his experience and expertise, also disappeared into the western part of Java. Reading these accounts of people going missing while in search of the missing certainly made me and my companion shudder, and wonder if we'd survive Baltimore and ever return home. As the holiday season came, and Christmas trees were placed in front of city hall, no reports had been received from the retired professor. The Baltimore

Board of Tourism, which oversees the sister cities programs, decided it would be best to focus its energy on the upcoming holiday arts festival, and so abandoned the possibility of establishing a relationship with the world's most populous Muslim nation. Their search efforts completely ceased a week before the Christmas holiday began.

UNDERCOOKED

WE WERE NOT THE FIRST FROM OUR HOMETOWN to immigrate to Baltimore—a certain two men and a woman had traveled there a few years before us. They visited a notable seafood restaurant in Butcher's Hill on their first night in the city. They looked forward to a good meal, but the food was undercooked and the two men immediately experienced acute stomach pain. Under the spell of their intense disappointment with what their guide had touted as the city's finest culinary offering (and their remarkable drunkenness), all three marched into the kitchen, grabbed a man in a white coat whom they took to be the head chef, and stabbed him with one of his own knives. The next morning, the bodies of the two men and the one woman were found floating in the harbor, where they had apparently drowned themselves out of remorse for their hasty response to the undercooked meal. A report in the newspaper back home explained that all three had traveled to Baltimore to conduct an extensive study of progressive education methods. The man they had stabbed, a husband and father of an infant daughter, was, in fact, the sous chef, and he died from organ failure before he even reached the hospital, while their intended victim, the head chef, went on to open several successful restaurants, both in Baltimore and Philadelphia.

RAGS

IN BOLTON HILL we heard of a dog, an Alsatian, who had been adopted by a new family because his original owners had found his expressions and wails too melancholy and depressing; he would urinate on the window seat, or in the yard in warmer weather, and weep just audibly until the sun rose and some time later, until the family who owned him was suffering from such depression that it became necessary to put the dog up for adoption. It was true: the constant glumness the dog carried with him had made the lives of his human family miserable. He was also known to escape the yard regularly, defecating on the neighbors' stoops and lying down to nap at busy intersections, which for many would have been cause enough to bring him back to the shelter. But his owners wanted to place him in a good home of their own choosing, so they chose to give him to a young couple in the neighborhood who were expecting their first baby, figuring the child might bring the dog some joy. For the first month at his new home, the Alsatian refused to come inside and spent every night quietly weeping in the garden. Once the baby was born, however, the dog entered the house immediately and without hesitation. During that first night, the dog, who was always called Rags, bit the sleeping infant, causing permanent damage to her eye and leading to his own death at the hands of animal control.

COINCIDENTAL FLIGHT PATHS

I N A SINGLE WEEK, shortly before the end of our stay in Baltimore, three of our friends, who all lived on the same block as we had, left their families (spouses and children) and moved from the city. These were the neighbors who made days bearable and reminded me of the existence of *purpose*, as the mission that brought us to Baltimore often eluded us during our year there. The father of five (moved to Nashville, Tennessee) felt that his voice would never be heard in his home. The mother who had never worked in a compensated job (moved to New York City) had stopped sleeping because she feared she couldn't withstand the loss of her husband and children, a constant possibility. The single mother of three (moved to Pennsylvania) called her sister to inform her that the children would be her responsibility, as she had lost a sense of duty toward them; they elicited a true indifference in her, and she understood intellectually that it is impossible to parent without feeling. All three fled because their domestic purposes could no longer be clearly described.

24

WENT DIRECTLY TO THE TRAIN STATION, having no good-byes to offer and no loose ends, one might say, to tie up. When I arrived, I was pleased to see that several more trains were scheduled to leave the station on that warm spring evening. I had no trouble getting a seat on an express train to a station near my hometown, and I knew that I'd be there before the end of the night, leaving Baltimore and my sister behind.

I had more than an hour to wait until my train's departure. Instead of sitting in the station's lobby, a grand construction that stood as testament to the city's nineteenth-century golden age, I walked out to the platform beside which my train was scheduled to board. I found an empty bench and I looked out at the quiet tracks.

Over the next few hours, a handful of trains eased their way in and out of the station. Nighttime trains seem to run with less urgency than their daytime counterparts, and their passengers similarly move with less anxiety. I watched dozens of people disembark, about to return to or arrive in Baltimore, a series of unforeseen experiences in that city awaiting them. At the same time, and what really intrigued me, were the dozens of people I watched boarding trains, as I would be shortly, and I speculated as to the permanence of each of their departures. Some might have planned only a short trip away from home, although that didn't guarantee they would ever come back; others might've meant to return in some far-off, unspecified time, and may have assumed the inevitability of that return beyond probability; and still others likely intended to never return again, but, I understood, probably would.

One train, waiting on the tracks across from where I expected my own to arrive, remained for an extended period. The passengers had, for the most part, boarded much earlier, except for a few stragglers who seemed surprised and relieved to find their train still waiting. Judging from the railroad employees, most of whom wore coveralls, climbing into and out of the train's engine car, the train was experiencing some technical malfunction, presumably a relatively minor one, as no announcement was made concerning its cancellation.

I watched the train and considered how this delay might affect the lasting nature of its passengers' various departures; as I considered this, I heard a voice calling from down the track. It was a voice that repeated two syllables, again and again, louder and louder, and which, as I expected, defined themselves as "Bar-ney," my name. During my final moments in Baltimore, I was being called. I stood up and walked toward the voice, which became clearer as I approached the rear of the train. Soon I recognized that unlike the one I heard in the warehouse, this voice was not that of a child, but of a woman. Her call wasn't plaintive, nor was it scared; it was a call of expectation, if not joy. I walked farther down the platform, the call intensifying all the while.

Finally I located the source in a specific car. The voice clearly came from within, but when I approached the car's windows, I could see no one inside who appeared to be shouting my name or any other. In fact, nobody inside the car appeared to hear the incessant call, or, if they did, they had all chosen to ignore it completely, and conducted themselves as all other sleepy and bored passengers waiting for the end of a long delay might: eating potato chips, looking at magazines they didn't want to read, and unsuccessfully trying to sleep without the rhythm of the moving train to lull them. I stepped back to see if the voice might be coming from somewhere else, but it was not.

Abandoning politeness, I pushed my face against the windows, hoping to overcome the obscurity of the tinted glass and the glare from the station's lights. What I saw was my own face staring back at me, reflected on the glass. My eyes struck me: there was fear in them, fear I didn't even know I was experiencing. I looked down and saw my mouth moving, opening and closing, struggling to produce the same sounds over and over, and quickly I realized those sounds were the same ones I'd been hearing, the two syllables of my own name. I pulled back, believing that I myself was the source of the call, but when I did, I saw that the face in the window wasn't mine, in fact, but one like mine, except with the curves and slopes of a woman's aspect.

I ran for the train car door, as I understood immediately that my choice to abandon the search had allowed me to find her. My sister was right here before me. I stepped into the train car and the voice stopped. In its place was the ringing bell of the last boarding call. They had finally repaired the engine, and the train was preparing for departure. The insistent ringing freed me from the spell of hearing my name, and I stopped. I turned to see the train car door sliding closed behind me. Without hesitation I kicked my foot forward, triggering the door's safety mechanism and forcing it to open.

I stepped back onto the platform and returned to my bench. I continued to wait for my train, my back to the one I had just abandoned. I refused to turn around until I could no longer hear it moving down the tracks, slowly picking up speed on its way out of Baltimore.

THE CAMPAIGN AGAINST MARATHONING

I WOKE EARLY ONE SUNDAY, at the insistence of a friend, to observe Baltimore's annual marathon. While the event, at least for onlookers, was mostly characterized by tedium, I did observe one marathoner of interest: a salesman from Mount Washington. After completing the marathon in less than four hours, he said he had accomplished the number one item on his things-to-do-before-I-die list. Having announced this, he then had to admit that crossing the finish line was the greatest letdown of his life thus far, a feeling with which I can sympathize, as I too was once driven by impractical, corporate-sponsored physical competitions, having completed an Olympic-distance triathlon, and was practically crushed by the dearth of fruit produced by my labor. But I rebounded quickly and used my new-found cycling acumen as a means of efficient transportation. The Mount Washington salesman, on the other hand, sought retribution for the time and energy wasted on the marathon and, according to my friend, dedicated his weekends to attending various organized footraces and heckling the participants as they crossed the finish line. He also distributed hand-printed booklets to sponsors, explaining the wastefulness of the culture they were encouraging by funding these races. The effort the salesman put into his antimarathon campaign distracted him from his demanding job, which eventually led to him getting fired for dwindling sales figures. Incidentally, his crusade must have had little effect, as the Baltimore Marathon had its highest participation ever the following year, and the passion for the race was so great that heart attacks struck two runners, one of whom died.

SYMPATHETIC INTENTIONS

O N THE TRAIN TRACKS that run behind Baltimore's Penn Station, a conductor threw himself before a slowing train that was easing forward
just enough to crush him, because, as he stated in a final voicemail to his
wife, after a full career working for Amtrak, having earned the right to a
full pension, he could no longer abet people in the pointless practice of
shuttling from one place to another simply to consume things and stay
distracted until they died, and that, he said, was an accurate description
of every passenger whose ticket he checked. This argument was not unlike
that left in a suicide note written by my uncle almost twenty years ago, in
which he claimed, as a surgeon, that he could no longer continue practicing
new ways of prolonging the lives of those who continued on with no purpose but to avoid death. Dying, after all, his note claimed, was a legitimate
and often productive choice.

LATE SEASON

I N REMINGTON, CONCERNED NEIGHBORS who had not seen Mrs. Gross (an elderly woman who lived alone in a large house) in almost a week called the police to report their fears about her well-being. She was indeed found dead, her body still in a sitting position and the television still turned on and tuned to the Orioles game when the police entered the house. In her fingers, she clutched a soft and worn Orioles cap. She had actually settled down to watch the baseball game on an earlier night, the night when she had died. The Orioles lost that game, we determined from the box scores, and were officially eliminated from playoff contention with a loss the following night. The game playing on the television when the police found the woman's body was nothing more than a late September afterthought of a failed season. It was around this time that my companion and I began to silently wonder if our mission in Baltimore had progressed to a similar lame-duck stage.

THE MAN WHO FIRST WELCOMED US

IN A HOUSE NOT FAR FROM FEDERAL HILL, which I reached after a brisk walk from the north of the city and located with the guidance of several local residents, I paid an unannounced visit to Polares, a man who had contacted us not long after our arrival in Baltimore, a man who specifically suggested that our lost brother and sister were very likely to be found, even decades after they had gone missing. I rang his bell and waited several minutes. Then, just as I turned to leave, a young woman opened the door and quietly invited me inside. She instructed me to sit at the counter in the small kitchen, then disappeared up a back staircase. I heard whispers from above. I tried to remember if Polares had a daughter, or perhaps a son that had gotten married. The young woman returned to the kitchen and invited me to follow her upstairs, where she led me down a dark hallway and into a small and overheated bedroom. It took me several moments before I realized there was a body lying beneath the bedsheets, and a few more moments before I was relieved to see that the body was alive—it was an aged and sickly Polares who smiled at me, his mouth barely visible above the top of the sheet. I held one of his hands and told him what a joy it was to see him again; he could only nod in response, as he was too weak to speak. I sat with him, silent and reverent and almost happy. The sky grew dark as night came, but he kept his eyes open, trained on me, then on the bedroom door, and then on me. It was only when I could no longer stay awake that I left my sick friend's bedside. When I went back downstairs, I spoke with the young woman who had let me in, and she told me she was Polares's nurse, and that he had been very sick for many months, and, in fact, six weeks ago he had been given one month to live. As I rode out of Baltimore, I thought of Polares, the very person who had encouraged our exile and its palpable, if fleeting, sense of purpose, and wondered aloud if he had passed.

MANIFEST DESTINY

O N THE OCCASION THAT THE PEOPLE OF BALTIMORE trouble themselves
to welcome someone who visits their city with the intention of staying long enough to one day make the claim to *live* there, as they did in the
case of me and my companion, they always use a distancing hospitality, so
as to ensure that the visitors will never turn native, a method that is more
effective than cursing the interlopers (or spitting on them, or vandalizing
their rental properties). People like us immigrate to Baltimore out of admiration for a city where we believe we might find answers. Yet our presence
threatens the natives' solace, and, this being the case, we are dogged by our
neighbors' uneasiness until the day we decide to return to the towns we
came from. Those we left in Baltimore will scorn us for giving up on them,
and will presumably spread the word of their failed hospitality abroad.
Those Baltimoreans who cannot avoid discussing their memories of the
visitors who have left, because so many of their own shared experiences
involve these outsiders, address us only to disparage our characters (which
cannot be defended by we who are absent). The sad reality is that by black-
ening their memories of their visitors, they are ruining their chance to
overcome their own disappointments. They drove one particularly enlight-
ened visitor to Pittsburgh, a town that restored his hope in Baltimore. During my final days in Baltimore, he called me to say that he missed the city's
charm, and that he planned to return as soon as it was practically feasible.
Without hesitation, I told him to stay in Pennsylvania, pointing out the
failure of Baltimore to welcome any outsiders, and insisted that a return
would be the end of the hope that he had worked so hard to restore. (My
companion and I had come to understand that the chill we felt in Baltimore
was the one thing that might save us from being completely consumed by
our tragic quest.) Against my suggestion, he signed a lease in Baltimore

not one month later. On the morning that he returned, I stopped by his studio apartment to greet him, and he was so broken he couldn't even muster the spirit to get out of bed and say hello.

25

SHORTLY AFTER RETURNING HOME, I took a job in the public information division of an arts nonprofit, where I remained for many years because I was quite happy with the work, as it gave me the opportunity to talk to many different kinds of people, and, because of the organization that I represented, they were open and even enthusiastic about talking to me. The hours were reasonable, but I often worked late, not out of pressured obligation, but because I was eager to further the work of the foundation. On one such night, another colleague also stayed late, as we were crafting the language for an invitation to our holiday fundraiser and decided it would be best to get the cards printed up sooner rather than later. Satisfied with the copy that we had crafted, we both logged out of our computers and put on our coats. She and I talked about the daunting prospect of returning home late only to have to cook something to eat, and decided that our most prudent choice would be to get dinner at a local restaurant, a sort of diner-pub where we could enjoy a well-mixed and well-earned cocktail with our meals.

We drove separately to the restaurant, which we had visited on so many previous Wednesday nights, and sat ourselves in one of the many empty booths located along the back wall of the dining room. We gave the waitress our orders without the need for menus, then we sat back, able to enjoy a relaxed dinner with only the need for brief and unremarkable conversation. The sympathy that is forged by the quotidian experiences of the office allows for this ease and lack of anxiety, social and otherwise. When you eat with someone you know well, you can eat in relative peace.

I was feeling particularly content that evening, having finished a large project for the foundation, and having ingested a nice amount of steak and bourbon. My coworker felt the same, so we agreed to have one more cocktail before heading home to undoubtedly sleep very well. As we drank our second drinks, we mostly sat quietly and watched a late-season baseball game set on mute, playing above the bar. Neither team had a chance of making the playoffs, and the energy of the game seemed to reflect that fact.

My attention wandered down to the bar below the television, where a man sat on a stool that he seemed unable to keep in place, tipping one way and then another and, impossibly, never tipping over completely. I became rapt by his ability to come so close to falling and somehow right himself at the last possible moment, as if by complete chance. He then began to point at the television and say something to the bartender. I strained to hear—it seemed he was asking him to change the channel, to turn off the out-of-market game that no one cared about. I became intrigued not by what he was saying, but by the sound of his voice. It was one I had certainly heard before.

When she had finished her drink, my coworker stood and said good-night. She was going to head home before she became either drunk or exhausted. I said that was a good idea and told her I'd be doing the same momentarily. Once she had left the restaurant, I took the remainder of my drink down the bar, as I was interested in learning more about this odd, apparently drunk man. I seated myself with an empty stool between us, so as not to be too obvious in my curiosity. He immediately turned and said, "So you found me."

The voice was indeed perfectly familiar, as it was that of my companion, whom I had not seen for so many years. I had left Baltimore on the train that evening and, often to my surprise, never once returned. I slowly learned that I could remain occupied by other challenges and problems than that of my missing sister, and be distracted by the other impediments I faced each day. I often wondered if my friend had learned the same lessons, or if he was still bound up in his own investigation. And now he was sitting beside me in a restaurant in our hometown, less than a mile from where we first met.

His face was, of course, older, thicker, and harder, and I assumed mine was too. He was always a restless man, but he now appeared positively frenetic, rocking back and forth, pushing his overgrown and graying hair back from his forehead.

"I found you?" I asked him. It seemed more likely that he had found me, and I quickly began to consider that it was possible that he'd found me years before. Had I been living again under his eye, as I had for those months in Baltimore?

"Well here you are, sitting beside me," he said.

"Have you been following me? Watching me again? Is that how you've spent your years?"

He laughed and rocked the stool again, almost but not quite tipping it. "I wish it was. But you know where I've been."

"But you're not there now."

"Not now," he agreed.

My friend's eyes searched the room, darting from one spot to the next, looking at everyone and everything but me. Seeing him brought back instincts I had fought very hard to suppress. "Did you find him?" I asked. "Did you find them?"

He looked at me and smiled weakly. He began to slowly nod. "Of course I did."

The answer paralyzed me; it was the worst response I could have imagined.

"I've found them many times, again and again." He stood up and put on his coat. "And, I can assure you, I will find them again."

"Where are you going?"

"Now?"

"Are you going back?"

"Am I going back right now?"

"Yes."

"I hope not." And with that, he weaved his way toward the door.

"But you know it won't end," I called after him.

"That's right," he said, and pushed himself out the door and into the night.

I finished the last sip of my drink and mourned my defeated friend, confident in my resolve to stay away from that city. I couldn't help but laugh at my own blindness and pride.

ACKNOWLEDGMENTS

I DIDN'T WRITE THIS BOOK ALONE, I'd like to offer my sincerest gratitude to my friends who read this book in its various forms. Thank you to Mark Doten, Jane Elias, Kristen Iskandrian, Andy Moody, Edward Mullany, Adam Robinson, and Janice Shapiro for your insight and criticism, your inspiration, and your admonition. I am especially grateful to Lincoln Michel and Ginny Woods, who worked beside me and made sure this book didn't become another atrocity itself. And thank you to my editor, Anitra Budd, for seeing the story among the atrocities and allowing me to share that tale.

I'd like to thank the editors of the following publications, in which several of the atrocities first appeared:

"Daycare," "Easy," "An Accomplished Runner," "A New Friend in Atlantic City," "Beside the New Jersey Turnpike," "At the Tax Preparation Office," "Moral Balance," "The Stallion," and "Pilgrimage" appeared in *Atticus Review*, 2013.

"Sainthood," "Pro Bono," and "The Campaign against Marathoning" appeared in *The Florida Review*, 2012.

"An Accomplished Runner," "The Farmer's Daughter," "Holiday Traffic," and "Right Time, Right Place" appeared in *Big Lucks*, May 2012.

"Taken," "Sheldon Weathers," and "New Jersey" appeared in *Heavy Feather Review*, Spring 2012.

"A Husband and Wife," "An Unexpected Whim," "The God's Honest Truth," "Like My Mother," and "Domestic Unrest" appeared in *DIAGRAM*, August 2011.

"Before the Hitchcock Residence (Los Angeles, CA)," "Mother's Intuition," "On the Third Floor of Union Memorial Hospital," and "The Mouthy Drunk" appeared in *Gigantic*, May 2011.

"The Most Profitable Poetry Reading," "The Shut-In," and "Labor Policy" appeared in *Beecher's*, Spring 2011.

"Statute of Limitations" and "Civic Duty" appeared in *JMWW*, April 2011.

"The Famous Shortstop" and "Late Season" appeared in *Hobart*, April 2011.

"Cold Water," "Lab Tests," and "Lab Partners" appeared in *Wag's Revue*, March 2011.

"Guilt" appeared in *Matchbook*, March 2011.

"Coverage," "Extended Sentence," and "Security" appeared in the *Collagist*, February 2011.

"Factory Renaissance" appeared in *Everyday Genius*, January 2011.

"Salesman," "Fudderman's Folly," and "Labor Agreement" appeared in *Fix It Broken*, January 2011.

"The Swimmers" appeared in *Devil's Lake*, January 2011.

"Role Model" appeared in *Gone Lawn*, Issue 1, September 2010.

FUNDER ACKNOWLEDGMENTS

COFFEE HOUSE PRESS is an independent, nonprofit literary publisher. All of our books, including the one in your hands, are made possible through the generous support of grants and donations from corporate giving programs, state and federal support, family foundations, and many individuals that believe in the transformational power of literature. We receive major operating support from Amazon, the Bush Foundation, the Jerome Foundation, the McKnight Foundation, the National Endowment for the Arts—a federal agency, and Target. Our activity is also made possible by the voters of Minnesota through a Minnesota State Arts Board Operating Support grant, thanks to a legislative appropriation from the arts and cultural heritage fund. Special project support for this title was received from a Jerome Foundation 50th Anniversary Grant.

Coffee House Press receives additional support from many anonymous donors; the Elmer L. & Eleanor J. Andersen Foundation; the David & Mary Anderson Family Foundation; The Alexander Family Fund; the E. Thomas Binger and Rebecca Rand Fund of the Minneapolis Foundation; the Patrick and Aimee Butler Family Foundation; the Buuck Family Foundation; the Carolyn Foundation; Dorsey & Whitney Foundation; Fredrikson & Byron, P.A.; the Lenfestey Family Foundation; the Nash Foundation; the Rehael Fund of the Minneapolis Foundation; the Schwab Charitable Fund; Schwegman, Lundberg, Woessner & Kluth, P.A.; the Private Client Reserve of US Bank; the Archie D. & Bertha H. Walker Foundation; and the Wells Fargo Foundation of Minnesota.

Members of Coffee House Press's Publisher's Circle also provide support through significant contributions to our annual giving campaign. With the understanding that a strong financial base is necessary to meet the challenges and opportunities that arise each year, this group plays a crucial role in the success of our mission. Recent Publisher's Circle members include many Anonymous Donors, Mr. & Mrs. Rand L. Alexander, Suzanne Allen, Patricia Beithon, Bill Berkson & Connie Lewallen, Claire Casey, Jane Dalrymple-Hollo, Mary Ebert & Paul Stembler, Chris Fischbach & Katie

Dublinski, Katharine Freeman, Sally French, Jeffrey Hom, Stephen & Isabel Keating, Allan & Cinda Kornblum, Jocelyn Hale & Glenn Miller, Roger Hale & Nor Hall, Kenneth Kahn & Susan Dicker, Kathryn & Dean Koutsky, Leslie Larson Maheras, Jim & Susan Lenfestey, Sarah Lutman, Carol & Aaron Mack, George Mack, Joshua Mack, Gillian McCain, Mary McDermid, Sjur Midness & Briar Andresen, Peter Nelson & Jennifer Swenson, Rebecca Rand, Jeffrey Sugerman & Sarah Schultz, Nan Swid, Patricia Tilton, Marjorie Welish, Stu Wilson & Melissa Barker, Warren Woessner & Iris Freeman, and Margaret Wurtele.

COLOPHON

The Baltimore Atrocities was designed at Coffee House Press, in the historic Grain Belt Brewery's Bottling House near downtown Minneapolis. The text is set in Iowan Old Style with Frutiger Bold used as display.

JOHN DERMOT WOODS RECOMMENDS THESE COFFEE HOUSE PRESS BOOKS

SLEIGHT
KIRSTEN KASCHOCK

"It's increasingly rare for any book to really surprise you. *Sleight* does more: it astonishes. A rigorous, unsentimental, strange and beautiful work."
—CHINA MIÉVILLE

THE FIRST FLAG
SARAH FOX

"It has been a long time since I have been so excited about a book of poems the way I am for Sarah Fox's *The First Flag*. The poems are some of the most human-animal poems I have read, disarming and beautiful, scary because they are about us, honest and rough, intelligent and real." —MATTHEW DICKMAN

SUBMERGENCE
J. M. LEDGARD

"An extraordinary fusion of science and lyricism . . . . [A] darkly gleaming novel about love, deserts, oceans, lust and terror."
—ALAN CHEUSE, *NPR*

LEAVING THE ATOCHA STATION
BEN LERNER

"One of the funniest (and truest) novels I know of by a writer of his generation. . . . [A] dazzlingly good novel." —LORIN STEIN, *THE NEW YORK REVIEW OF BOOKS*

THE DEVIL'S SNAKE CURVE
JOSH OSTERGAARD

"Expansive and inventive . . . a challenging reconsideration of a game that used to be called the national pastime."
—*STAR TRIBUNE*

JOHN DERMOT WOODS is a writer and cartoonist living in Brooklyn, NY. He is the author of a collection of comics, *Activities* (Publishing Genius, 2013), and two previous illustrated novels, *No One Told Me I Was Going to Disappear* (with J. A. Tyler) and *The Complete Collection of people, places & things*. He and Lincoln Michel created the funny comic strip, *Animals in Midlife Crises*, for the *Rumpus*.